O1

- BOOK 1 -

wish

the OTHERWORLD
- BOOK 1 -

wish

VICTORIA HARRIS

Wish
Copyright © 2021 Victoria Harris

Published by Ogham Publishing

Paperback: 978-1-9196126-0-7

Illustrations: Asur Misoa
Book production: Julie Karen Hodgins

For Theo & Cara

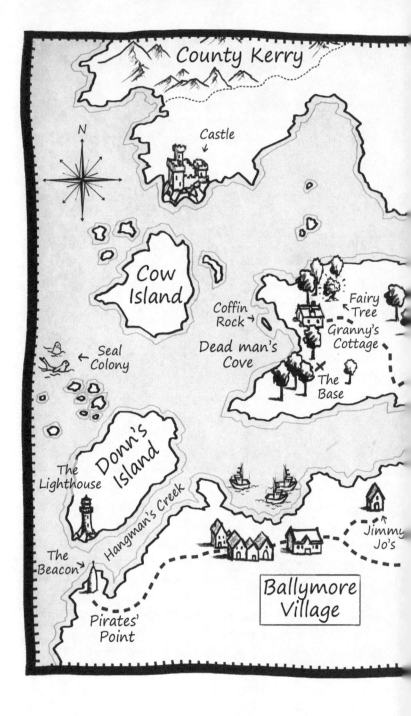

- ONE -

A Bridge to
Another World

ACCORDING TO IRISH FOLKLORE, if you crossed the ancient stone bridge to Inish Roga, you'd enter another world.

I gazed out the window as the hills rolled by, some all but swallowed up in low-hanging storm clouds. A single, fat drop of rain splashed against the glass. Just one, for now. But I could tell the clouds would unleash them all soon.

Aunt Jackie hummed under her breath as she flipped on the turn signal while Granny fiddled with the heat. Next to me, Bri stared straight ahead, the dark circles under her eyes even more prominent than usual. I was sure I didn't look much better.

This will be good for us, I told myself for the hundredth time in the last few days. *Being at Granny's will help.*

But thinking something wasn't quite the same as believing it.

1

"Treep hasn't changed much since your last visit, has it, girls?" Granny said with forced cheer. In the mirror, her eyes crinkled as she looked from Bri to me.

"Nope!" I tried to match her tone and failed dismally.

Unsurprisingly, Bri didn't respond. My younger sister hadn't said a word since Dad's disappearance.

Granny was right about the town of Treep though. Connolly's pub, with its peeling green paint and weather-beaten orange chairs sitting forlornly outside, hadn't changed a bit. Even the giant dangling spider next to the entrance was the same one I remembered from the last time I was here at Halloween.

Treep loved Halloween. The roadside was lined with home-made scarecrows donning straw-stuffed shirts and trousers, Halloween ghouls adorned with frightening, grotesque masks, witches' hats and broomsticks and cauldrons. Roughly carved pumpkins in all shapes and sizes were scattered outside low garden walls, and ghosts made of white netting hung from the trees, fluttering with increasing intensity as the wind picked up speed.

The heat was really blasting now, and I was getting uncomfortably warm in my red puffy coat.

Bri traced her finger across her window, leaving a streak in the condensation. Her curly chestnut hair dusted her shoulders, framing her doll-like features. It needed a good brushing, to be honest. Normally, Mom wouldn't let her go out with her hair in such a tangle. But Mom could barely get out of bed, much less brush her eight-year-old daughter's hair. It was all she could do to take care of our little brother, barely a week old.

If I was being honest, Mom couldn't even do that right now, which was why my maternal grandparents were staying with her and the baby. A few days after Dad left, Pop Pop gently explained to Bri and me that Mom wasn't feeling very well.

"She just needs time," he told us softly. "Time and the right medication. She'll be right as rain soon enough, my dears. And in the meantime, this little trip will be good for you two."

This will be good for us, I repeated again in my mind. But in my heart, I couldn't understand how splitting up our already fractured family could be anything but bad. Guilt slithered over my bones like vines, and I closed my eyes to fight off the thought that had been taunting me all week.

This is all your fault.

A sharp pang of pain in my head made me gasp. Startled, I realized I'd been tugging at a strand of copper hair so hard I managed to yank it right out. Bri turned her haunted stare on me, and I flushed, hastily brushing the stray hair away.

With Treep falling away behind us, the tarmac narrowed and the trees seemed to inch closer, bony branches reaching out like witch fingers to scrape the top of the car. My pulse quickened as Aunt Jackie slowed for the next turn, because I knew what came next. A narrow road that climbed up, up, up, until we reached the top of the hill and emerged from the trees to see the view that never failed to knock the breath from my lungs.

The stone causeway stretched out before us, arching over the choppy waters to an island so green, it shone like an emerald between the gray sky and sea.

"Let's leave the world behind."

I was startled to hear the words Dad always whispered when we reached this part of the drive. It took me a moment to realize they came from my mouth.

If Granny or Aunt Jackie heard me, they chose not to respond. Aunt Jackie stepped lightly on the brakes as we drove downhill and onto the bridge. Bri rolled her window down a crack, and after a moment, so did I. The crisp, salty Irish air filled my lungs, and once again, my heart panged with sadness as I heard Dad's voice in my mind.

This air is the freshest in Ireland, he always told us, right after inhaling in a deep, exaggerated way that caused Bri and me to giggle. *Air that's traveled unhindered all the way across the Atlantic Ocean.*

The breeze ruffled my hair as I took in the seagulls surfing the wind overhead. I could see waves lapping against tiny rocky islets as curlews searched for food on the mudflats. Our car trundled across the bridge, and memories of Dad surfaced in my mind like seals coming up for a much-needed breath.

The last time I'd been here, it was a beautiful summer's day. The sun shone brightly in a clear blue sky as Dad led Bri and me over an emerald-green carpet of clover. I remembered watching my steps so carefully, looking out for bumblebees. Then my gaze landed on something, and my heart skipped a beat.

"Dad! Dad, look!" I shouted, barely able to contain my excitement.

Dad turned, brow furrowed. "What is it, Cara?"

"I found another one!" Bending over, I plucked out the four-leaf clover and waved it over my head triumphantly. "I *always* find one!"

His face softened into a warm smile. "I told you, Cara! You have fairy magic."

I giggled with delight. Next to Dad, Bri crossed her arms, her mouth pulling down at the corners.

"So do I," she said, her gaze searching the grass. After a moment, her eyes teared up. "Don't I?"

"Of course you do, sweetheart!" Dad lifted Bri up and twirled her around, causing her to squeal with delight. "Your gift is different from your sister's, but you have one all right." He set her down, and Bri flashed me a smug smile.

I ignored her, tucking the four-leaf clover behind my ear.

Eventually, we came to a small cove. Dad found a nice flat rock to sit on while Bri and I mucked about, delirious with abandon.

"Keep an eye out for fairy stones!" he called, his booming voice audible even over the crashing waves.

Bri and I looked, at one another, wide-eyed. Then we ran back toward Dad, eager to hear more. We loved when Dad told us stories about the Fae. Not just because he was an amazing storyteller but because he really seemed to believe every word. He made it sound like a whole magical world was out there, and we could find it if we just looked hard enough.

"What's a fairy stone?" Bri asked, sitting cross-legged at his feet.

I lingered behind, trying not to seem overly interested. I figured I was probably getting too old for such tall tales, after all.

"It's a magical stone, often found on beaches just like this one, identifiable by a hole in its center," Dad said, gazing around as if expecting to spot one any moment.

Bri and I looked, too. Crispy seaweed lay strewn on the pebbles nearby. I kicked away a patch, releasing several flitty bugs and a pungent smell but no fairy stone.

"Why does it have a hole?" Bri asked.

Dad looked out at the sea thoughtfully. "The old stories say that if you look through it, you can see into the Otherworld of the fairies."

Bri drew in a deep breath, her eyes shining with delight. I couldn't help but feel a little awed by the idea, too.

"Have you ever seen one?" I asked before I could stop myself.

Dad paused only for a moment. "Yes," he said, and Bri's mouth fell open. "Right here on this very beach."

"Where is it? Can we see it?" Bri cried, leaping to her feet.

"I wish I could show you," Dad said with a sigh. "But sadly, I lost it long ago." His eyes twinkled as he took in our disappointed expressions. "But if you're lucky, a merrow might leave one on the beach for you to find!"

"What's a merrow?" I asked.

"A sea fairy! The fairies are always looking for someone to help them in their quest. You never really know why the fairies pick you to find one, but they say it's always for good reason."

My skepticism returned in full force. "Quest?" I repeated, arching an eyebrow.

"That's right!" Dad stood up, brushing dirt off the back of his jeans. "A quest to stop the darkness from overtaking the world!"

His voice had taken on that over dramatic tone it did when he really got into a story, and I couldn't help but snicker a little.

Bri, however, looked completely enthralled as Dad continued.

"The fairies live in a realm of light, which is full of sparkle—a pure life-force energy. But there are other realms, too. Like the one where the Formors rule. The Formors gain power by spreading darkness. They're relentless, and if they ever succeed, all other realms—including ours—will be in grave danger."

I wasn't laughing anymore.

Dad gazed out at the horizon, his expression now distant.

Bri gnawed on a fingernail. "How can the Formors be stopped?"

"They can never be completely stopped," Dad said softly.

I moved closer, not wanting to miss a single word.

"You see, just like in our realm, some darkness will always exist. That's why it's important to maintain the balance, to recognize the truth."

Even the wind seemed to grow still at his words. I shivered slightly, rubbing my arms and feeling the goose bumps that had broken out.

Suddenly, Dad seemed to snap back to the present. He threw his arm around Bri and squeezed her, causing her to relax and giggle.

"You remember who you're named after, Bri?"

"The Fae queen Brigid!" Bri cried without hesitation.

"That's right! Brigid is full of fairy sparkle and helps keep our world balanced. Many, many years ago, the Formors put a dark spell on her that caused her to be bound by time and the seasons . . . and imprisoned her sparkle in a rock."

"Imprisoned her sparkle?" I repeated again, trying not to sound too doubtful.

Dad nodded. "In Hag's Rock, as a matter of fact—it's not too far from here, on a clifftop down that way." He pointed to a series of cliffs in the not-too-far distance. "When Brigid is born on Halloween, her sparkle is released from the rock, and she grows older and stronger through spring and summer just like everything in the seasons, working hard to help the earthly realm before her strength fades again."

His voice took an overly sinister tone—not really scary but more silly, like the narrator of an old monster movie.

"In the winter, Brigid is known as the Bow . . . an old lady with withered blue skin, hiding her face under a black-hooded cape. People often fear her at this time, because she's in the shadow realm, with the darkness obscuring her light."

Bri let out a high-pitched, nervous giggle.

Dad pulled her closer and winked at me.

I tried to suppress a grin as I asked, "Have you ever seen her?"

"Not myself, no. But I know a local man who said he saw her once. She was brushing her long, silvery hair with a white shell comb. And others have said they heard her cries just before a death in the family . . . or that she knocked on their door three times. The Bow is only seen during that time of year where the veil is very thin between the realms, like Halloween."

Bri ran her fingers through her curls absentmindedly. "She has a shell comb?"

"Yes! That's her treasure," Dad told her. "Sometimes the darkness hides it from her, and woe betide any human who dares to take it! All of the fairies' most important treasures lay hidden from the Formors. Four of those treasures have an enormous amount of sparkle, which is why the Formors want to destroy them. But Brigid . . ." Here, Dad paused and planted a quick kiss on top of Bri's head, and she beamed. "Well, Brigid will stop at nothing to bring more sparkle into the world, because it helps to dispel the darkness and bring balance to the earth."

"But she has less power in winter," I said, no longer trying to hide my interest in the story. "Right?"

Dad nodded, solemn again. "That's when the darkness spreads. Most humans have forgotten their sparkle, hypnotized by the darkness that obscures it. Only a human with the right amount of inner sparkle can bring the Fae treasures back into the earthly realm before it's too late."

"Can we help Brigid bring back the sparkle, Dad?" Bri asked.

"We can sure try," he replied with a chuckle.

The car jolted as we passed over a bump, wrenching me from the memory. Aunt Jackie said something, but her words sounded muddled. Darkness crept in on the edges of my vision, and everything seemed to slide out of focus. The world went mute save for the sound of my own shallow breath.

What is happening to me?

I was paralyzed, a black void rushing past me—or maybe I was falling into it, pitching face-first into darkness. I couldn't hear, see, taste, smell, touch . . . but gradually, I became aware of another sense. A new sense. It was fuzzy at first then sharpened onto something in the void.

A shadow. A horrible, sinister shape that was somehow even darker than the void itself, and it was speeding toward me like the jagged maw of a shark closing in on its prey.

"No!"

The word was ripped from my throat, and just like that, the world came back into focus: the car, Aunt Jackie, Granny, Bri, the rain that was now pelting against the windows, the world beyond a blur of gray and green.

Only Bri seemed to have heard me. She placed a hand on mine, giving me a curious look. I just shook my head, yanking my hand away. I didn't want her to feel how badly my fingers were trembling.

I had no idea how to describe what had just happened. But whatever that darkness was, it had shaken loose an answer to a question I'd been asking ever since Dad had disappeared. *Why* had he chosen to go on a hike in the mountains just days after Mom gave birth? Why had he picked such a difficult trail? What could have been so urgent that it had torn him away from his family right when we needed to be together more than ever?

Was it possible it actually had something to do with the Fae? With the Formors and the darkness?

Remember your thoughts have power, Cara. Pay attention to them.

It was one of the last things Dad had said to me. Tears stung my eyes, and I squeezed them shut as the car rumbled along. I bit my lip hard until I tasted the metallic tang of blood on my tongue.

Mom had had a rough pregnancy, and because Dad worked so much, I'd helped out a lot at home. I hadn't minded at all, except I had to skip a lot of tennis practice. We had a big tournament coming up, and Dad told me after dinner the night before that he couldn't be there.

It was too much. "I'm already nervous because I've missed so much practice!" I cried, stopping just short of adding, *Thanks to you.* "I'm not prepared. I thought you'd be there to cheer me on!" I'd felt so abandoned.

Dad took my hands in his and squeezed. "Some things are out of our control," he said calmly. "But the way you think about things is not. Remember, your thoughts have power, Cara. Pay attention to them."

A flush crept up my neck. "But I need you there!" I pleaded.

"I'm so sorry, Cara. But I know you'll be great. You're a warrior! Strong as a rock."

He gave me a kiss on the cheek and left. I'd stared at the door long after it closed behind him, fists clenched at my sides. I was hurt. I was angry.

And I wished him *gone.*

It was a wicked thought. One that came true. Because Dad *was* gone, vanished somewhere in the mountains, and after three days, the rescue team hasn't seen so much as a sign of him.

Most humans have forgotten their sparkle . . . hypnotized by the darkness that obscures it.

"Granny?" My voice came out breathless and high.

In the passenger seat, Granny turned to look at me. "Yes, dear?"

"I . . . is . . ." I paused, trying to find the words, trying not to sound panicked. "Do you remember all the old stories Dad used to tell us? About the Formors, and the . . . the darkness?"

For the briefest of seconds, I thought I saw a shadow flicker over Granny's face. Then she smiled at me, her eyes sparkling.

"Oh, yes. Those silly old stories. You girls used to love hearing them when you were little, didn't you?"

I forced a smile and nodded, all at once feeling foolish. The moment Granny faced front again, I closed my eyes.

Silly old stories. Fantasies. Folklore. *Magic isn't real.*

Yet I couldn't help thinking that whatever just happened to me had been very, very real. There was a darkness inside of me. The kind of darkness Dad always warned me about.

I didn't listen. And now he was gone.

I wasn't a warrior. I wasn't strong. The things I wished about Dad were wicked, which meant only one thing—I was, too.

- TWO -

Ard Na Mara

I COULDN'T EVEN APPRECIATE the lush green grass and gently rolling hills as our car wended its way along the perimeter of the island on a narrow, bumpy road. More than anything, I wanted to get out of the car. To be alone for a moment, to try and process . . . whatever that was, that terrifying darkness I'd just experienced.

I crossed my fingers that we wouldn't meet another car trundling along from the opposite direction. If that happened, Aunt Jackie would be forced to reverse backward until she found a wide enough spot to get out of the other car's way.

But we were lucky this time, reaching the end of the road without encountering another vehicle. I breathed a sigh of relief when I spotted the open metal gate with the sign that read *ARD NA MARA,* marking the outskirts of the land Granny owned.

As Aunt Jackie tapped on the brakes, I unbuckled my seatbelt. The rain had stopped for now, but I didn't care much if I got wet. "I'll walk from here, if that's okay!" I said, attempting to sound as normal as possible. "Stretch my legs."

Granny turned to smile at me. "Of course, dear. We'll see you back at the house."

Relieved, I hopped out and slammed the door. I waved as the car ambled past the gates and down the muddy track. Then, alone at last, I exhaled and took in my surroundings.

All around me, trees swayed, their leaves whispering secrets. Through the thicket, I could just make out a view of the gray sea. I walked slowly across the grass, taking care not to get my sneakers muddy. I could never remember exactly how many acres of headland Granny owned, but it was a lot. A long time ago, it was a goat farm. When Dad was little, he would help his father with the cheese production. But Grandpa died before Dad was even a teenager, and that was the end of it. Now, the land is a remote wilderness of beaches, native woodland, and wildflower meadows.

I gazed up at the trees, trying to appreciate the autumn colors. But the leaves weren't the ruby red and bright gold I remembered. They were pale yellow, sallow, as if the life had been drained out of them.

An image flashed in my mind. Dad curled up on the ground, cold and alone, the wind whipping around him, his skin deathly pale and his eyes open and—

Stop.

I froze for a moment, forcing that awful image out of my head. Dad was missing. But he wasn't dead. I had to believe that. I *had* to.

I continued through the trees and after some time, I reached the shore. I walked all the way to the water's edge until there was nothing but sea stretched out in front of me. Crouching down, I selected a flat gray rock about the size of my palm.

You're a warrior. You are strong as a rock.

I let out a choked, bitter laugh as I stood up. Squeezing the rock, I gazed out at the water and blinked away a few hot tears. Then, rearing back, I hurled the rock as far as I could.

Years of tennis practice had really strengthened my arms, and the rock made a beautiful archway, way out over the waves before finally landing with a barely audible splash.

It felt so satisfying, I immediately searched for another, bigger rock. And then another, and another.

Too bad I hadn't been able to serve like this during my tennis tournament. It was a poor performance, to say the least. My teammates didn't blame me outright, but I could tell they were disappointed. They probably figured I would beat myself up about it more than anyone else ever could.

That was the worst part though. Because normally, they'd be right. I took tennis very seriously. But after the tournament, I couldn't even bring myself to care about how poorly we'd done. With Mom hardly acting like herself and Dad increasingly unavailable, I couldn't bring myself to care much about anything at all.

I thought things couldn't get any worse. Then Mom had gotten the phone call from the hotel in County Kerry where Dad had been staying.

They said he'd left his hotel room to climb Carrauntoohil on Sunday and he had never returned. Pop Pop had driven Mom, Bri, and me to Kerry while Nan watched our baby brother. It had been the longest car ride of my life.

Dad's open bag was still on his hotel bed, surrounded by crumpled clothes. His shaving foam and aftershave sat next to the sink in the bathroom, filling the place with Dad's scent. It all felt like a cruel joke, like at any moment Dad would leap out of the closet and laugh at our surprised expressions.

Mom had locked herself in his bathroom. Bri and I could hear her sobbing. Pop Pop was on the phone all afternoon, and at some point, Aunt Jackie and Connor showed up. The whole time, I felt strangely detached. Like I was watching a movie. Like this wasn't actually happening to me.

An ache in my arm from the exertion brought me back to the present. I turned my back on the sea and began the walk to Granny's house. I knew the path well, because Dad would take Bri and me down to the beach every day when we visited. It was a long, winding track uphill, past rust-colored scrub and a thick wooded area. At the brow of the hill, I wandered off the path and made my way through the violet heather. I loved the view from here, with the white beacon at the entrance of Ballymore Harbor pointing up to the sky like a finger.

I made my way back to the path. I could see the wooded area up ahead that marked the border between Granny's land and the cattle farm that Aunt Jackie and Uncle Pat owned. I pictured their farmhouse, gray with a bright green door. My cousin Connor had painted it himself last year.

The thought of Connor brought a real smile to my face for the first time that day. Connor was barely a year older than me at thirteen, and he'd always been my best friend. Suddenly, I couldn't wait to see him.

I picked up my pace, feeling slightly cheered. But then the wind carried a faint sound that caused me to stop in my tracks. Angry voices. Shouting.

Quietly, I made my way to the woods and slipped between the trees, keeping out of sight. Granny's white stone farmhouse came into view. I could see Granny outside talking to some-one tall and bulky, a stark contrast to her fragile frame. Aunt Jackie and Bri were nowhere to be seen.

I crept as close as I dared then squatted behind a bramble bush. I was still too far to hear what they were saying, but moving any closer would all but guarantee that Granny would spot me. The man had his back to me, but he was gesticulating wildly, his arms punctuating his shouts with fierce jabs at the air. When Granny shook her head, he lunged forward and grabbed her arm, yanking her forward.

I gasped, every muscle in my body going tense. But Granny pulled her arm away and gave him a cold look. When she turned and walked briskly inside the house, the man roared something after her, waving a pointed finger in the air. Then he turned and marched toward a beat-up red van I hadn't even noticed, muttering under his breath. He jumped in the driver's seat and slammed the door. I blinked as the engine rumbled to life. I'd seen that van in Ballymore before.

I got to my feet, hoping to catch a glimpse of the man's face as he turned out of the driveway. But the van lurched forward faster than I'd expected. I leaped back onto the muddy verge, my heart pounding wildly as the van sped past me. For a split second, I locked eyes with the driver, and my stomach flipped over.

One of his eyes was covered with a dirty black patch. His face was wrinkled and weather-beaten, and his wispy, peppery hair was pulled into a ponytail. When he saw me, his mouth curled into a crooked grin.

Then he was gone, the van rumbling over the crest of the hill and vanishing from sight.

"The fisherman," I said out loud. That was what Connor and I called him, even though we knew his name was Frank. He told us off once, shouted at us when we were sitting on the harbor wall minding our own business. He swore at us, and his anger had frightened me. The only other place I'd ever seen him was at the pub, propped up at the bar with a pint. He was sullen and quiet most of the time, but when his temper got the better of him, it was a scary sight.

I pictured the way he'd grabbed Granny's arm, and I shivered. What had he been so angry about? Why was he even here in the first place? As far as I could remember, Granny had never even mentioned the fisherman.

I jogged down the path toward the farmhouse. As I crossed the yard, a whisper nearly made me jump out of my skin.

"Cara."

I spun in a circle, gazing around wildly. For a brief, terrifying moment, I imagined Frank sneaking up on me with that wicked smirk and one cruel, glaring eye. But no one was there.

No *person,* anyway.

My gaze perched on the small, thorny tree in a clearing. *My fairy tree,* Granny called it, and she kept it covered in brightly colored rags and little trinkets that flashed in the sunlight.

It took me a moment to spot the robin amongst all the décor. Its fiery red breast fit in well with all the jewel-toned strips of cloth, its feathers fluttering ever so slightly in the breeze.

And its beady black eye was fixed on me.

There was tons of wildlife around Granny's farm. On the surface of it, there was nothing unusual about the robin. But something about the way it stared at me so fixedly unnerved me. And then there was the whisper, the sound of my name.

Had this robin . . . *talked*? Had it called my name?

No, I told myself immediately, giving myself a little shake. That was ridiculous.

But I *had* heard my name. And this creature was the only living thing I could see.

I thought of that awful episode in the car. That moment when everything had gone dark and I had tipped into a void, a horrible darkness opening up like the jaws of some terrible creature who wanted to swallow me whole.

Turning, I ran for the farmhouse.

Granny had left the front door open a crack, and when I stepped inside, the familiar scent of burning wood from the stove enveloped me like a warm embrace. I made my way to the kitchen, where I could hear the simmering, crackling sounds of something cooking on the stove.

The back door was open, but the kitchen was empty. Then I heard the muffled sound of Granny's voice coming from the sitting room. Hurrying over, I pressed my ear to the door and listened as hard as I could.

"It's the *curse* . . . yes, him. I have to stop him. We could all be in danger . . ." Granny spoke in low, hushed tones, and I couldn't catch every word. "I know a way . . . If I don't do something, it could be a disaster . . . had enough grief around here."

At that moment, a gust of wind caught the back door. It slammed shut with an almighty *bang,* the metal key inside the lock clattering to the stone floor. I hurried over and picked it up just as Granny entered the kitchen.

"Cara! How was your walk?" Granny asked, crossing the kitchen to pull me into a quick hug. I breathed in the scent of lavender and wool before she released me.

"Good." I watched as she headed to the stove, pulled the lid off the stockpot, and inspected the soup bubbling away inside.

Aunt Jackie entered from the sitting room, giving me a smile.

I smiled back, trying to work up the courage to ask what they had been talking about. *Curse . . . disaster . . . grief.*

Dread tied a knot around my insides. "Granny," I said hesitantly. "When I walked in, I heard . . . I thought I heard you say something about a—" I couldn't bring myself to say *curse,* so instead, I said, "Disaster?"

For the briefest of seconds, Granny froze. Then she turned to look at me, her long pewter plait swinging over her shoulder. "You must have misheard, dear. I'm quite sure I didn't say anything like that. Aunt Jackie and I were just having a chat about . . .

well, about everything our family's going through right now. I'm expecting a call from mountain rescue today. They promised an update about your dad." Her tone had turned sympathetic.

Swallowing hard, I stared at the key still clutched in my palm. I didn't want to talk about Dad. Or Mom, for that matter. Instead, I focused on the curious charm attached to the key ring—a cord with a circular piece of dark blue glass.

"What is this?" I asked, holding it up. "The charm?"

Granny smiled before turning her attention back to the soup. "It's an evil eye."

I nearly dropped the key ring. "An evil eye?"

"That's right. For protection against curses."

My eyes widened. I glanced at Aunt Jackie, but she had busied herself setting silverware out on the table. I examined the charm closer, and my stomach gave a little lurch when I saw the chip. "Oh, it's broken!"

"Is it, now?" Wiping her hands on her apron, Granny walked over and took the charm from me. A flicker of worry passed over her face so quickly, I wondered whether I'd imagined it. "Just a wee chip," she said, slipping the key into her apron pocket. "Nothing to worry about."

"But what about the curse?" The words burst from me before I could stop myself.

Granny gave me a sharp look, and Aunt Jackie dropped a soup spoon, which landed on the table with a metallic clatter.

"What?" Granny asked.

I swallowed hard, trying to muster the courage to tell her what I'd overheard her say. *It's the curse.* "Y-you said . . . you said it's for protection against curses," I said, chickening out.

Granny's expression softened. She gave an easy laugh and returned to the stove. "Just a little superstition, Cara. I wasn't being serious."

Aunt Jackie cleared her throat. "Trek through a bit of mud, did you?" she asked, gesturing to my feet. I glanced down and saw splatters of mud all over my sneakers.

"Oh, I was—" I glanced up. "I was coming up the path when a van came roaring out of the driveway, so I had to jump out of the way."

Granny made a disgusted sound. "Frank," she muttered, stirring the soup vigorously. "Reckless man, he is."

"Frank?" I repeated innocently. "Isn't he that fisherman from Ballymore?"

"That's right."

"What was he doing here?" I pulled out a chair and sat, still trying to sound only mildly curious. I suspected Granny wouldn't be pleased if she knew I'd heard them argue and witnessed Frank grab her so violently.

Granny began ladling steaming soup into bowls. "Oh, he wanted to talk about a factory they're planning to build in

Skullageen. A microplastic factory. Awful idea, especially so close to the sea—it's sure to pollute the waters."

I frowned slightly, watching as Granny set two bowls down on the table. As if someone had summoned her, Bri appeared in the doorway. She walked silently to the table and sat between Aunt Jackie and me.

"A microplastic factory would be terrible for the environment," Aunt Jackie told me.

For a moment, I wasn't sure why she'd felt the need to explain that. I was on the recycling committee at school. I knew plastic was terrible for the environment. Everyone did.

Then I realized my brow was all scrunched up like I was confused. Because I *was* confused—not about the factory but about Frank. Why would he be raging at Granny about a microplastic factory?

I attempted to clear my expression as Granny continued talking.

"The worst part is they had to cut down a small woodland for the site. It's always been zoned as a green belt, but a few years ago, it was changed. Funny business got that rezoned, if you ask me. I started a campaign against it and got quite a petition together, but unfortunately, it still looks like it's going to get the go-ahead."

"So, Frank wants the factory built, then?" Aunt Jackie asked.

Granny snorted. "Goodness, no. He's furious about the whole thing."

"Is that why he was yelling?" I blurted out before I could stop myself.

Granny's eyebrows shot up, but I saw the corner of her mouth pulling up in a smile. She began slicing a fresh loaf of bread, her silver bangles jangling.

"The company is trying to buy it from him. Brian Lalor's putting all sorts of pressure on Frank—so are his supporters, and he's got a lot of them. Money talks around here, you know."

"Is Frank going to sell?" I asked.

Granny and Aunt Jackie exchanged an amused look. "Why the interest in all this, Cara?" Aunt Jackie asked with a laugh. "I would think talk of rezoning and land permits is dull stuff for someone your age!"

I shrugged, ducking my head and blowing ripples across my soup. I watched them hit the side of the bowl, picturing the water lapping onto shore. Then I imagined the water turning to sludge, spreading up the shore and covering the rocks in slime, the grass going brown and brittle, the trees withering . . .

A flare of anger sparked up in my chest. Maybe Frank's fury was understandable, even if Granny was an undeserving target. A microplastic factory would change the entire area, including the island—and not in a good way at all.

An uncomfortable silence hung over the kitchen. I decided to change the subject.

"Is Connor coming over?" I asked Aunt Jackie before lifting a spoonful of hot soup to my lips.

Aunt Jackie gave me a sympathetic smile. "Not this afternoon, I'm afraid," she replied. "He's helping Pat with the cattle. We've lost quite a few of them recently. Awful case of blackleg."

I lowered my spoon. "Blackleg?"

"Terrible disease," Aunt Jackie said, shaking her head. "Starts out with depression, loss of appetite, then the limbs start to swell and—" She stopped, glancing at Bri, who was staring down at her bowl of untouched soup. "Well, it's not exactly something we want to chat about over lunch!" she said in an overly cheery voice. "Pat and Connor will get the cattle healthy again, no doubt about that. In fact—"

But whatever Aunt Jackie was about to say was lost to what happened next.

Granny reached for a slice of bread, her elbow knocking the rim of her bowl. At the exact same instant—maybe even a split second earlier—Bri lunged forward, arms outstretched. Granny let out a cry of surprise as her bowl of soup tipped off the table . . .

. . . and landed neatly in Bri's waiting hands.

For a moment, the four of us sat there as still as statues. Granny with her hand still reaching for the bread, Aunt Jackie with her mouth open mid sentence, me with my spoon halfway to my mouth. And Bri, half out of her chair, cupping Granny's bowl in her palms, the soup gently sloshing from side to side.

Finally, Bri set the bowl back on the table. It was as if a spell had been broken. I lowered my spoon, staring at my sister as Aunt Jackie let out a fluttery little laugh.

"What reflexes!" she said, smiling at Bri. "That was quite a save."

"Indeed it was," murmured Granny. Was it my imagination, or was her expression almost suspicious as she studied my sister?

I turned my attention back to Bri. She stared down at her own bowl, stirring her soup listlessly with her spoon.

Second sight. I closed my eyes as yet another Dad memory surfaced. We'd been right here in this very kitchen, Bri and I snacking on apples with thick slices of cheddar as Dad told us about our supposed fairy magic.

"You have second sight, my dear," he said, tickling Bri under the chin and making her giggle. "The ability to see things before they happen."

"What about me?" I'd asked eagerly around a mouthful of apple.

Dad winked at me. "I believe you can sense emotions, Cara. It's a very special power."

I frowned thoughtfully. "How do you know we have these powers?"

"I've seen the signs in both of you," Dad said, grabbing a piece of cheese. "You'll have to work on developing your powers though. It takes time and practice."

"How do I do that?" I set down my apple, all my attention on Dad.

He tilted his head and considered this as he ate his cheese. "Granny's old radio," he said at last. "You know how when you're looking for music, you have to keep fiddling with the knobs until you get a good, clear sound?" When I nodded, Dad smiled at me. "It's like that. You catch a little bit of your power, and you tune in to it. Slowly, carefully. Takes a bit of practice, but you'll get there."

I'd understood, sort of. But that was years ago. Bri and I had been so young, and eventually, I realized all Dad's talk about powers and fairies was just make-believe, just like Mom always said.

Now, though, I remembered that strange sensation in the car, the feeling of tipping into darkness and speeding toward some blurred, shadowy thing I felt more than saw. Had I been "tuning in," as Dad suggested? If I had tried harder, *slowly, carefully,* could I have locked into some emotion that wasn't even mine?

The shrill ring of the telephone ripped me from my dark thoughts. I nearly dropped my spoon as Granny stood and hurried to the phone.

She picked it up and answered with a breathless, "Hello?"

Aunt Jackie, Bri, and I stared at her face, trying to read her expression. My heart thudded painfully in my chest, beating out one word over and over again.

Dad. Dad. Dad.

"I see . . . I see. Yes, thank you. Do let us know the moment you—yes, of course. Take care."

She hung up the phone and turned to face us with a bracing smile.

"No sign of Michael yet," she said briskly. "But they've learned he told another climber he was going to take the Devil's Ladder route."

"That's good news," Aunt Jackie said. "Now they know where to search!"

Granny nodded, but something in her eyes made my stomach sink. "Indeed. It may be slow going though. The day Michael went hiking, the weather changed rather quickly. The route would've been quite treacherous. Still is, they said."

"Ah." Aunt Jackie looked as though she was casting about for something positive to say.

But I didn't want to hear it. I was tired of all the false hope adults had been trying to force Bri and me to believe in ever since Dad had gone missing. I was tired of the fake cheer and statements like *I'm sure he'll turn up,* as if anyone could be sure of such a thing.

"Maybe there really is a curse." I didn't mean to say it out loud. The words fell like heavy rocks in a pond.

Granny and Aunt Jackie stared at me, startled.

"Cara," said Granny, and I heard a slight tremor in her voice. "Don't be silly, now. You'll scare your sister."

I looked at Bri. She gazed directly back at me, her eyes dark and haunted.

At last, I shrugged and took another bite of my soup. But I saw the look Granny and Aunt Jackie exchanged. And I knew what I'd heard them talking about, as much as they tried to deny it. *It's the curse . . . it could be a disaster.*

They were keeping something from me. And I was going to find out what.

- THREE -

Balor of the Evil Eye

AFTER FINISHING MY SOUP, I excused myself quickly and headed up to the room Bri and I always shared when we stayed with Granny. I turned everything over in my mind as I walked up the stairs: Granny's encounter with Frank, the plastic factory, the cattle and their blackleg.

But mostly, I thought about Dad. The Devil's Ladder route. *Treacherous.*

And I thought about the curse.

I pushed open the door to my room. My suitcase was just inside, and I heaved it onto my bed. Only then did I notice the purple gift bag resting against my pillow. *Granny.*

Instantly, I felt guilty for how sullen I'd been at supper. Granny always had presents for Bri and me when we came to visit. She was so thoughtful.

Hastily, I emptied the contents onto the pastel pink patchwork quilt. Despite everything, I couldn't help but smile at the sight of the lined journal with the silver Irish knot on the front cover, along with a ballpoint pen with a purple feather at the end, just like an old-fashioned quill.

"Granny!" I hollered over my shoulder toward my open door. "Thank you. I love them!"

I was halfway finished with putting my clothes in the dresser when Bri appeared. She hurried over to her bed on the other side of the room while I found a few spare hangers in the closet for my jumpers.

"Squawk!"

Gasping, I whirled around.

Bri stood a few feet from me, her hand covered in something black and fluffy. It had legs, feet, and a large beak.

"Oh!" I said, hand on my chest. "Is that a bird? A bird puppet?"

Bri smiled. "Squawk! Squawk-squawk!"

Tears stung my eyes as I watched the beak open and close. This was the first time I'd heard Bri's voice in days. It was hoarse, probably because she hadn't used it in so long, but the familiarity of it made me realize just how much I had missed hearing her speak.

"Looks like you have another present," I said, pointing at the pink gift bag on her bed. I watched as Bri pulled out an art pad and colored pencils. She hugged them to her chest and, with the bird still firmly on her hand, hurtled out of the room. I heard her footsteps pounding down the stairs and smiled to myself.

A moment later, Granny knocked on the open door. "Glad you like them," she said, eyes twinkling as she pointed to the journal and pen. "And I'm assuming Bri liked her raven?"

"She talked!" I exclaimed, zipping up my now-empty suitcase. "Well, squawked. But still! Maybe the puppet will help her talk for real."

Granny nodded. "That's what I'm hoping. She'll talk to it—and it will talk to her. Ravens have always been important familiars for those with special sight."

"Familiars?" I asked, setting my suitcase in the closet and shutting the door.

"Animals sent to help those who work with sparkle. They're like a guide—and a protector." Granny gave me a little wink. "Like my Hugo."

I giggled. "Your hedgehog is your familiar?"

"But of course!" Granny widened her eyes in a way that told me she was kidding.

But as she headed down the hall toward her room, I couldn't help wondering whether she was only pretending to joke. Dad was always fervent in his belief in the fairies and their magic. Even when Mom teased him mercilessly about how silly it all sounded, Dad would just smile and shrug and kiss her on the cheek. Was it possible Granny believed, too? But if she did, why would she pretend not to?

I left the room, closing the door quietly behind me. Down the hall, I could hear Granny moving around in her own room. I turned right and headed to the study at the end of the corridor.

Granny's study had always been my favorite room in the house. It was lit by lamplight, giving the whole room a soft, golden glow that was just bright enough to read by comfortably. The best part was the wall-to-wall bookcases, crammed to bursting with worn old books. Granny had a big collection of Irish folklore, in particular. I'd spent countless hours curled up in her armchair near the window, reading to my heart's content.

A book lay open on the armchair. I picked it up and sat down, sinking into the soft, worn cushions. I glanced at the title on the cover: *THE STONE OF DESTINY.*

Something about the phrase itched at the back of my mind. I'd heard it before, but between Dad's stories and all the books I'd read, that was no surprise. I flipped through the pages, skimming the contents. My eyes paused on the word *Formors.* I remembered Dad's words.

The Formors gain power by spreading darkness. They're relentless, and if they ever succeed, all other realms—including ours—will be in grave danger.

I continued skimming, but I was paying closer attention now. *The Stone of Destiny is one of the treasures of the Fae . . . contains sparkle, a great power . . . some believe it sits on the hill of Tara, but that is not the original stone. The true Stone of Destiny lies hidden by the Fae.*

I flipped ahead, but there seemed to be nothing about where the stone was actually hidden. Sighing, I set the book on the side table next to the armchair.

A small, black journal already lay there. Curious, I picked it up and opened to the first page. Two words were scrawled in Granny's handwriting.

Druid Magic.

My pulse quickened. I glanced at the door, listening for the sound of approaching footsteps, but the house was quiet. I turned the page, reading as fast as I could, my stomach sinking further with every word I read in my grandmother's hand.

Everyone has sparkle, that pure light that resides inside us. But some people's sparkle is more concealed. Shadowed, clouded, obscured by dark thoughts.

Druids are magicians who work with sparkle, and most help those who are full of darkness. But there is one whom the Fae fear. A Druid who uses dark magic to create thought enchantments that increase the darkness. A Druid who manipulates the earthly realm. He forged an alliance with the Formors and is committed to helping them find and destroy the Stone of Destiny.

He is called Ignis.

His shadow army has been growing, made up of terrible evil creatures that feed off negative energy. The Pooka, a shape-shifting goblin, is one of his favorites. This creature most often takes the form of a huge dog to accompany the Formor army, but it can change into anything a person fears.

Creatures like this are attracted to the darkness within us. But we can fight them by connecting to our sparkle. There are also protection spells that may be useful against Ignis.

The words blurred before my eyes, darkness creeping up in the corners of my vision. Dimly, I was aware that this felt like what had happened in the car, and for a few seconds I was paralyzed with fear. I didn't want to fall into that void again. I didn't want to face that monstrous darkness.

You catch a little bit of your power, and you tune in to it. Slowly, carefully.

I heard Dad's voice as clearly as if he were right next to me. Calm began to settle over me, and I focused on him with all my might. His kind, twinkling eyes, his warm smile . . . after a moment, I swore I could even smell his cologne.

Dad? Where are you?

I heard someone call my name distantly. But it wasn't Dad. The darkness began to dissipate, and the study slowly came back into focus.

After a moment, Granny's voice sounded from down the hall. "Cara? Could you come here for a moment?"

Gasping, I slammed the journal shut and shot to my feet. "Coming!" I called back, hurrying out of the study. I was still shaken by what had just happened. Was it just a powerful memory? Or had I actually connected with Dad for a moment?

I found Granny in her room, bent over Hugo's cage.

She glanced up at me as I entered. "Would you mind closing the door?" she asked. "I was hoping to have a private chat."

Swallowing hard, I closed the door obediently. "About what?"

Granny poured food pellets from a glass jar into Hugo's bowl. The hedgehog waited patiently until she'd finished before scurrying over. I couldn't help but smile as he noisily crunched his dinner.

"About Bri," Granny replied, and my smile faded. "When exactly did she stop speaking?"

"When Dad disappeared," I replied uneasily.

"Yes, but when *exactly*?" Granny probed. "How much time passed after he left for the hike before Bri went silent? When was the last time you heard her say anything?"

I frowned, thinking hard. There had been so much going on, with Mom's worsening condition and the near-constant wails of a newborn baby. I tried to conjure up a memory of Bri talking to me, to Pop Pop, to Mom . . . When I came up blank, I searched further back in my memory. The day Dad had left, when I'd been so worried about my tennis tournament. Had Bri and I spoken at all that day?

Guilt wrenched my insides. "I can't remember," I admitted. "But I don't think I heard her talk at all on the day Dad left."

Granny nodded thoughtfully as she screwed the lid back on the jar of food pellets.

Suddenly, I saw what she was getting at. "Oh. She stopped speaking *before* Dad was . . . before he . . ." My voice grew thick, and I took a deep breath. "Before he'd really disappeared. Before we knew something was wrong."

"Perhaps," Granny said, placing the jar on a shelf. "I asked your grandparents when I rang yesterday. They said they couldn't recall her saying a word since the day he left." When she caught sight of my expression, she forced a smile. "But of course, you were all so preoccupied with your mom and the baby, it's entirely possible you just didn't notice!"

I nodded as Granny crossed the room to her bathroom, closing the door behind her. But deep down, I knew that wasn't true. Bri had gone mute the moment Dad had left, as if she'd known he wasn't coming back.

Second sight.

My breath quickened as I pictured Bri lunging out of her chair a split second before Granny had even knocked her bowl over. Did Granny believe Bri had fairy magic the way Dad had? Could my sister's second sight be real?

And if it were, had she seen what happened to Dad on that hike?

The thought of Bri having a vision of something so terrible happening to Dad that she couldn't even speak broke my heart. A shiver raced up my back, and I crossed my arms tightly over my chest and crouched next to Hugo's cage.

The brown and gray hedgehog had finished his dinner and was now toddling over to the little nest of blanket strips that was his bed. Up close, I could see how much he'd aged since the last time I'd visited. He moved stiffly as he turned in slow circles on top of the bed, like a dog trying to find just the right position.

"Poor old thing," I said, reaching through the open top of the cage to stroke his spiky back.

Hugo stiffened then stood upright and glared at me. "Never touch a hedgehog attempting to hibernate, missy!"

I screamed, clapping my hands over my mouth and leaning away.

The hedgehog fell back to all fours, still grumbling under his breath. He curled up on his bed, and after a moment, his breathing slowed.

I stared at him, hands still pressed firmly over my mouth. What in the world had just happened?

The bathroom door flew open. Granny stood there in her robe, gazing at me worriedly.

"Cara? Something wrong?"

I dropped my hands to my sides, my mouth opening and closing. "I . . . um . . ." I stammered. "I went to pet Hugo, and he . . ."

He talked.

I couldn't say it. Granny would think I was losing my mind. She might be right, too. Between the strange incident in the car, the robin whispering my name, that connection with Dad in the study, and now a hedgehog chewing me out, I was beginning to question my own sanity.

"And I pricked my finger a little on one of his spikes," I finished at last. "It didn't really hurt though. Just startled me."

"He's a prickly little fellow," Granny replied with a grin. "*Brr* . . . it's getting chilly in this house! Let's get a nice fire going."

～ა

After the sunset and darkness fell over the woods surrounding the farmhouse, Bri and I changed into our pajamas. By the time we settled down in front of the fireplace with mugs of hot chocolate, I'd managed to convince myself that I had simply imagined Hugo speaking. I was tired, and grieving, and scared, I told myself firmly. That was all there was to it.

As the flames crackled and danced merrily over the logs, Granny lowered herself stiffly into her chair. She took a sip from her mug of hot lemon and ginger tea and smiled at Bri. "I see you've brought a friend?"

Bri's raven puppet let out a soft squawk.

Granny chuckled to herself, reaching for a tissue. She blew her nose then tucked the tissue into her sleeve.

"You know, girls," she said gently. "When your father was little, there was nothing he loved better on a night like this than a good story."

I sat up straighter, pulling the afghan quilt on the couch tighter around me. "A story about the Fae?"

Granny placed her feet on the footstool. She coughed into her fist before nodding. "Naturally."

I glanced at Bri, who was stroking the raven. "Will you tell us one now?" I asked Granny.

She hesitated only a moment. "Of course. I'll tell you one of his favorites. It's about the Formors."

Bri's dark eyes settled on Granny, her expression suddenly intent. I swallowed hard, trying not to picture that awful, dark void as Granny began the tale.

"The Formors came to Ireland from the underworld a long, long time ago. They brought darkness with them, along with a desire to rule over this world. One evening, the Formor king's son, Balor, was spying on his father's Druids from a castle window. They were performing a magical spell in a stone circle on a hill for his father. When they finished their ritual and left, Balor was overcome with curiosity. He crept up to the pot that was simmering on the hot stones in the middle of the circle. Slowly, he lifted the lid to peer inside . . ." Granny paused, and for a moment, the only sound was the wind whistling outside.

I held my breath, rapt with attention.

"Poisonous enchanted fumes hissed from the pot and filled Balor's eyes," Granny continued, her voice softer now, more distant. "It warped his eyes until they became one, a single, blind, evil eye right in the middle of his forehead. This eye was so full of darkness that Balor had to keep it closed at all times because to look upon someone with that eye would kill them where they stood."

I shivered, suddenly regretting asking for a story.

Bri sat completely motionless. She didn't so much as blink.

"Years later, when Balor became king, he wanted to rule over all the peaceful beings who resided in Ireland. These were a magical fairy race called the Sidhe, or the Fae, as they're more commonly known. They were full of a light so bright and pure, it sparkled. Balor sought to claim their sparkle and destroy their race. He built a huge army of shadow creatures to terrorize the Fae. Years of battles ensued, until one day, Lugh, the leader of the Fae, was preparing to battle Balor with his army of light warriors. Before the battle, he asked his familiar—a magical raven—for help."

I glanced up at Granny, startled. Her eyes were half-closed now, almost as if she were in a trance. Bri reached for her art pad and pencils as Granny began to chant.

"Raven Corwin come to me
Hear my call, beside me be
Residing at the healing well
Where the Sidhe spirits dwell
Protector of our sparkle bright
Guide us through your onyx flight."

Granny let out a soft, almost inaudible sigh. The room had grown dim, and I noticed the flames in the fireplace were dying out. Bri's pencil flew over her art pad, filling the room with a faint *scritch-scratch* sound. I pulled my blanket closer as Granny continued.

"Corwin flew ahead of Lugh's army to see Balor approaching and returned to warn Lugh. While this gave Lugh a head start, the battle that ensued was immense, and many Fae were lost. Eventually, Lugh saw his opportunity to defeat Balor. He shot a special talisman full of sparkle from a catapult straight into his evil eye. This dispelled the shadows, casting Balor and the rest of the Formor army back into the dark realms instantly. Ever since, they say that whenever there is a thunderstorm, it is Balor and Lugh still battling with one another."

BANG! A violent gust of wind slammed the shutters against the house. The three of us jumped, startled, and Bri dropped her pencil. Then Granny placed a hand on her chest and let out a laugh that was half-wheeze.

"Well, that's one way to end a story," she joked, reaching out to pull the chain on the lamp next to her chair. The soft, golden light filled the room, and I relaxed slightly. "Cara, dear, would you mind fetching a few more logs for the fire?"

"Sure." I threw off the blanket and stood, stretching. At the front door, I swapped my slippers for welly boots, pulled on my coat, and went outside.

I shuffled across the yard toward the woodshed, still thinking about the story Granny had told. The front door banged again behind me, and I glanced over my shoulder to see Bri hurrying to the fairy tree. The raven puppet was still securely attached to her left hand, a piece of paper clutched tightly in her right.

The wind picked up again, throwing up a whirl of pale yellow leaves in front of me and nearly knocking me right off my feet. I caught myself, turning away from the garage . . . and found myself looking at the small, dilapidated shed next to it.

A shiver ran down my spine, but this time it had nothing to do with the cold. There was no sound coming from the shed, yet I could have sworn I heard something—or sensed something. Before I knew it, I was hurrying over to it.

The door squeaked as I entered. I blinked, waiting for my eyes to adjust to this new level of darkness. Granny had always been a hoarder, but you'd never know it from the neat, cozy farmhouse. She kept all her old junk out here. I squeezed past cardboard boxes, gardening tools, various farm machinery that looked as though it had seen better days. Chipped garden pots and broken bikes were heaped in piles. I wondered whether one of the bikes was Dad's from his childhood.

A loud creak followed by a *SLAM* caused me to jump. I spun around and saw that the wind had blown the door shut.

I pulled my mobile out of my coat pocket and switched the flashlight on, sweeping it in a wide circle around the stacks of junk. The wind howled through the cracks of the woodshed as I moved deeper inside.

Dimly, I wondered what in the world I was doing in here. My feet felt like ice pops, Granny was no doubt waiting for the firewood, and I had no idea what I was even looking for.

But I *was* looking for something. It was almost like an invisible beacon was drawing me toward it.

A glimmer caught my eye at the bottom of a pile of old toys. Hurrying forward, I dropped to my knees and began moving things aside—a broken trike, metal toy cars, a teddy with a ripped head, parts of a train set. At last, underneath an old board game, I found a beat-up silver box with a sticker on top. I pulled it out carefully and saw the name *Michael O'Reilly* written in pen along the side. My heart leaped into my throat.

Dad.

I set down my phone and shook the box gently. *Clunk-clunk-clunk.* Fingers trembling, I pried open the lid and peered inside. For a moment, I couldn't breathe.

A smooth brown stone lay there. A stone with a large hole right in the middle and a red cord threaded through it. Tentatively, I touched the stone then picked it up.

Keep an eye out for fairy stones! My eyes brimmed with tears as I heard Dad's teasing voice. He told Bri and me he had found a fairy stone once but lost it. Could this be the stone he was talking about?

And was it really a *fairy* stone?

I slipped the cord around my neck and pressed the stone to my chest. A choked sob escaped my throat, and I closed my eyes. I thought of that connection I'd felt with Dad in the study, and I tried with all my might to feel it again. *Please. Please, Dad . . .*

Nothing. Desperate, I picked up my phone, found Dad's number, and tapped *Call.* I pressed the phone to my ear as it rang once, twice, three times before the automated response began. My shoulders slumped as I ended the call.

Then a new sound reached my ears. A distant wailing that made me shudder. Suddenly, I pictured Bri at the fairy tree and leaped to my feet.

"Bri?" I called frantically as I raced out of the woodshed and toward the tree. "Bri, are you . . ."

The words died in my throat. There was no sign of Bri in the yard. I glanced in the living room window and spotted Granny dozing in her armchair. I stood there, torn on what to do next. The wailing had ceased. It might have been an animal. Bri might have simply gone to bed.

A *thwap-thwap-thwap* sound caught my attention. I saw a piece of paper on the lowest branch of the fairy tree, flapping in the wind. The stark white stood out among all the colorful ribbons and trinkets. That certainly hadn't been there before.

I moved closer and realized with a jolt that someone had stabbed it right through the center with the branch. And it wasn't any old piece of paper. It was from Bri's art pad. I remembered the way she'd clutched it in her fist as she'd crossed the yard. Maybe this was what she had been drawing during Granny's story.

Nervously, I pulled the paper from the branch and unfolded it. My stomach lurched with fear. In black pencil, with heavy, almost violent strokes, Bri had drawn a hooded figure standing on a rock. The figure had no face, but I could almost feel a set of piercing eyes watching me.

"Aaahhhhhhheeeeeeeeeeeahhhhhhhhhh . . ."

The terrible keening sound started up again, and all the hairs on my arms and neck stood up straight. It was coming from the woods.

The urge to flee inside the house was almost impossible to resist. But as I turned, I caught sight of the muddy path—and the small footprints leading straight into the trees.

My sister was in the woods. Was she the one wailing? Or was she looking for the wailing thing? Both thoughts were equally terrifying, but either way, there was no hiding in the house now.

Shoving the paper into my coat pocket, I flipped on my phone's flashlight and hurried into the woods after her.

- FOUR -

The Bow

PLEASE DON'T BE HURT, *Bri. Please don't be hurt.*

I ran through the woods as fast as my wellies would allow, jumping over a few fallen logs and doing my best to avoid the deeper patches of mud. The wailing grew louder, but so did another sound—waves crashing onto rocks.

The wails were coming from the shore.

At last, I burst out of the woods and slowed, ignoring the stitch in my side and staring wildly up and down the beach. The soft glow of the moon cast strange shadows on the terrain as I moved toward the awful noise, stumbling over rough grass and slipping over a few rocks. As I drew closer to a cove, the wailing seemed to increase in volume.

It wasn't coming from inside the cove though. Carefully, I made my way over the rocky headland around the cove to the beach on the other side. The tide was very low, and I struggled to keep my balance on the slippery pebbles and patches of slimy seaweed.

My relief at finally stepping on sand was short-lived when I spotted a small figure walking slowly out to sea.

"Bri!" I screamed, running flat-out for my sister. But she didn't so much as flinch. It was as if she hadn't even heard me. As I ran, my gaze moved from Bri to the water beyond, the jagged shape of an enormous rock standing tall among the waves. *Coffin Rock,* I thought, my stomach lurching. That was what Connor and I had named it years ago, when Uncle Pat told us they used to bring the coffins of the dead from Cow Island by boat since they didn't have a graveyard. They brought them in at high tide and rested them on a giant, flat rock to wait for low tide so they could take their cargo over the bridge and on to Crag graveyard on the mainland.

As I gazed at the rock, my eyes came more into focus . . . and rested on the dark silhouette perched on top.

A seal, I told myself, but deep down, I knew this was no seal. This was the figure Bri had drawn in her art pad. This was the source of that awful wailing sound. But what *was* it?

The old stories say that if you look through it, you can see into the Otherworld of the fairies.

I stumbled to a halt, pulling the red cord out from under my coat. Shaking from head to toe, I held Dad's stone to my eye and peered through the hole.

What happened next was so disorienting, it took me a moment to understand what I was looking at. The stone magnified my view; I felt as if I was hurtling through the hole toward the creature at lightning speed, even as I stood still. And now, up close, I found myself staring in horror at a waif-like figure, hunched over and dressed in black. A dark hood covered its face, and one bony, blue-gray hand was caressing its long gray hair, its fingernails so long they had curled in on themselves.

"The Bow," I whispered, frozen to the spot in fear.

As if it had heard me, the creature raised its head. Its eyes, resting in dark sunken hollows, were balls of light. It let out another ear-piercing wail.

I dropped the fairy stone, and it thumped against my chest in tandem with my heart as I began to run again.

Bri was still making her way through the shallow water toward Coffin Rock.

"Bri, *stop!*" I scrambled as fast as I could toward my sister as the Bow continued to keen. The sand between the rocks was wet and sludgy. My foot caught in a patch of seaweed and I fell, banging my knee on the edge of a rock. Pain shot up my leg, but I ignored it as I pulled myself up.

Bri was almost at Coffin Rock now. She came to a halt, raven puppet dangling at her side, staring up at the Bow as if transfixed. Without stopping, I lifted the stone to my eye again. The Bow turned to Bri, stretching out her bony arms.

Her hood fell back to reveal a bluish, prune-like face, twisted and contorted, mouth open like a festering wound as her bony hands reached for my sister.

"*No!*" I lunged the last few feet and grabbed Bri's arm, yanking her back just in time.

The Bow let out a deafening screech. I spun around, ignoring Bri's cry as I pulled her back across the rocks and onto the shore. We ran back through the woods to the farmhouse, the Bow's wails falling farther behind us with every step.

I slowed to a halt on the porch, letting go of Bri's arm. We stood there, panting heavily and holding our sides.

"Was that—" I said at last, my voice scratchy and hoarse. "Was that the Bow?"

Bri didn't meet my gaze.

Frustrated, I walked to the other side of the porch and peered in the living room window.

"Granny's sleeping," I said shortly, still struggling to catch my breath. "She doesn't need to know you . . . you ran off like that. Just wait here while I get the firewood, and we'll go inside together."

Bri nodded once, her eyes on her feet. I marched over to the garage, gathered up a few logs, and returned to the porch. Bri opened the front door, and we went inside together.

Granny's head jerked up when I tossed the logs onto the fire. "Oh! I must've dozed off." She blinked, looking from me to my sister. "Goodness, you're both so pale and sweaty. Are you feeling feverish?"

"We're fine," I said, probably too quickly. I shot a smile at Bri and hoped it didn't look forced. "We had a little game of hide-and-seek while I was getting the firewood, that's all."

"Ah." Granny lifted a hand to her mouth and yawned deeply. "Well, girls, I think it's getting to be my bedtime. Do you need anything? Extra blankets, perhaps?"

"No thanks." I gave Granny a quick hug. "See you in the morning."

"In the morning," Granny echoed, giving Bri a kiss on the cheek before padding out of the room.

Bri followed her, casting me an unreadable look before heading up the stairs.

I sank down into Granny's armchair and stared at the crackling fire. Now that Bri and I were safe, the reality of what had just happened was setting in.

The Bow had visited us.

A terrible sense of foreboding settled over me. I stroked the fairy stone hanging around my neck and tried to think. Should I have told Granny what I'd seen? Would she have believed it? Surely she would dismiss the Bow as another silly old story . . .

But the story she'd told Bri and me about the Formors hadn't been silly. And then there was the stuff in her journal, about Ignis and Druid magic. Not to mention the way she'd talked about that curse to Aunt Jackie.

Contrary to what she claimed, Granny took all of the folklore about the Fae very, very seriously.

Sliding off the armchair, I moved closer to the fire. But even as I held my hands out to the flames, I couldn't seem to warm up. Somewhere out there, Dad was on a mountain path, lost and cold. Aunt Jackie and Uncle Pat's cattle had blackleg, Mom was sick, Bri was mute . . .

Maybe my family really was cursed. And now, after seeing the Bow for myself, I had to face the fact that the Fae were real—and they might be involved in all of the terrible things that were happening.

And Granny *knew*. So why was she pretending not to?

- FIVE -

Away with
the Fairies

I AWOKE HOT AND CLAMMY at the same time, sweating beneath the pile of blankets. Morning light seeped through the blinds on the window. Squinting, I pushed off the blankets and sat up. My dreams had been dark and murky, and after a moment, the memory of last night returned.

My hand reached automatically for the cord around my neck, and I sighed with relief when my fingers found the stone.

The *fairy* stone, I reminded myself, that had shown me the Bow.

I pictured her blue face, her hollow eyes, and shivered despite the warmth. In the bright light of morning, the idea that I had actually seen the Bow last night seemed ridiculous. Was it possible I'd hallucinated that part?

I thought of Hugo chiding me and the robin whispering my name. My skin prickled unpleasantly. Either I was having an emotional breakdown . . . or all of it was real.

Of course, I hadn't been the only one to see the Bow.

I stood and crossed the room to my sister's bed. Her raven puppet lay on the floor next to her discarded dressing gown. As I sat on the edge of the bed, she let out a soft snore. Her dark hair was damp and plastered against her forehead. Frowning, I placed my hand there. It felt warm and sticky with sweat, but she wasn't feverish, at least.

"Bri?" I said softly. "Are you okay?"

She fidgeted, her eyes blinking open. Her gaze moved from me to the raven, and she stretched out an arm for the puppet.

"Here you go," I said, picking it up and placing it on her waiting hand. The raven's beak opened and closed as Bri let out a soft squawk. "Bri, why on earth did you go wandering off like that last night?"

She stared at me, her eyes like two pools of chocolate.

I sighed. "Were you sleepwalking?"

Silence.

"Could you see . . . her?"

Silence.

"Why did you go to her?"

"Squawk."

Startled, I watched as the raven puppet turned to look at Bri. They stared at each other for such a long time, I actually forgot she was controlling him. It really looked like they were having a silent conversation.

"Bri!" I said at last, frustrated.

With a sigh, Bri set the puppet down and reached for her dressing gown. She slipped her hand into the pocket and paused, eyeing me. Then she looked away and pulled her hand out, gripping something tightly in her fist. After a moment, she placed it on the duvet in between us. I stared at it, unable to believe what I was seeing.

A smooth white shell comb with three pointy teeth, glistening in the sunbeam from the window.

"The Bow's comb," I croaked. "You found it."

Bri slid the raven puppet back onto her hand. "Squawk."

Cold dread crept up my back as I remembered Dad's story. *That's her treasure. Sometimes the darkness hides it from her, and woe betide any human who dares to take it!*

"You were trying to give the comb back to the Bow," I whispered.

"Squawk."

"Oh, Bri . . . and I stopped you!"

I buried my face in my hands. My pulse beat a frantic rhythm in my throat. I took three long, deep breaths and tried to steady myself. Then I looked up at my sister.

"Well then, there's only one thing to do. We have to return it."

❧

Granny was hanging up the phone as Bri and I entered the kitchen.

"News about Dad?" I asked immediately, hope and fear filling me in equal measure.

"No, dear," Granny said with a sympathetic look. "That was your Aunt Jackie. She said you're welcome to join them for breakfast, and then she's bringing Connor into Ballymore if you'd like to tag along."

At the mention of Connor, I suddenly felt infinitely better. "Yeah, that'd be great!"

Bri and I trudged over to Connor's house in silence. We had hidden the Bow's comb in the back of my sock drawer. My reasoning was that we couldn't risk losing it by carrying it around with us, and Bri seemed to agree.

I kept glancing at Bri out of the corner of my eye. She had sketched the Bow in her art pad before she'd even seen her. And the way she'd walked toward Coffin Rock as if under a spell had been disturbing, to say the least. I was worried about my sister.

But I was also deeply frustrated with her. I needed her to tell me what was going on, but she couldn't—or wouldn't—say a word.

I couldn't wait to tell Connor everything. It would be a relief to talk to someone who would actually talk back.

"Hiya, my loves!" Aunt Jackie said cheerfully as Bri and I entered through the kitchen door. She was scrubbing dishes stacked high in the Belfast sink, her bright, floaty skirt swaying around her ankles as she moved in time to Ed Sheeran's voice crooning from the radio. On the stove, a large pot of oatmeal simmered gently, filling the kitchen with the warm scent of cinnamon and nutmeg.

"Morning!" I replied, kicking off my wellies. Bri did the same, waving at Aunt Jackie with her raven. "Is Uncle Pat still here?"

"No, I'm afraid he was up and out before sunrise dealing with the cattle." Aunt Jackie let out a heavy sigh. "Unfortunately, we lost more of the herd last night."

"That's terrible," I said, suppressing a shiver. Last night, Bri had tried to return the Bow's comb, but I had stopped her. Was that why more cattle had died? Was it part of the curse?

"Cara! Bri!"

I turned as Connor walked into the kitchen, rubbing his eyes blearily. His hair was sticking up in all directions, and he was still wearing his pajamas.

"Hi, Connor!" I said, giving him a teasing grin. "Sleep in a little bit?"

Connor stifled a yawn before returning the smile. "Hey, I've been up at dawn every day this week helping Dad," he said, sitting down at the table. "He told me I could take this morning off."

I pulled up the chair next to him while Bri sat down on his other side.

Connor looked startled at the sight of the raven puppet. "What's that, Bri?" he asked.

An awkward silence fell. I swallowed hard, glancing from Connor to Aunt Jackie. She must have told him about Bri going mute, right?

Connor seemed to realize his mistake. "I, um . . ."

"It's her familiar," I rushed to explain, keeping my voice light. "You know, an animal sent by the Fae to protect her?"

Aunt Jackie began to set bowls of steaming oatmeal on the table, each topped with a small heap of diced apple and walnuts. "It's a big deal to get your familiar," she said, winking at Bri. "That raven must sense your inner sparkle."

Bri smiled down at her oatmeal, picking up her spoon with her free hand.

As Aunt Jackie went back to the dishes, I glanced at the raven and felt a pang of envy. It was ridiculous to be jealous of a puppet, of course. I knew Granny had given it to Bri in the hopes it would help her find her voice.

But I couldn't help thinking that the reason Bri had a familiar and I didn't was because she had sparkle, while I was lost in darkness.

"So, are you guys all set for Halloween?" Connor asked, digging into his oatmeal.

I shrugged. "Same costumes as last year. I'm gonna be a zombie tennis player. Bri's going as a skeleton. What about you?"

"Batman," Connor said cheerfully. "Sean's going as Robin. Want to come to Harry's party with us? Harry is going to DJ!"

I perked up at the thought of something as normal as a Halloween party. I liked Harry too. He was my older cousin Eoin's best friend.

"Sure!"

I glanced at Aunt Jackie. Her back was to us as she scrubbed the dishes, and I wasn't sure whether she could hear us over the sound of the radio and running water. Still, I didn't want to risk her overhearing me tell Connor I'd actually seen the Bow last night. She would no doubt tell Granny, and I didn't want anyone to know Bri and I had snuck off to the beach in the dead of night like that.

So instead, I focused on my oatmeal. It was sweet and spicy, and the soft apples and crunchy walnuts were the perfect topping. Connor started telling me about some video game he and his best friend Sean had gotten into recently, but I barely heard a word. In my head, I planned exactly what I would say to Connor about the comb and the Bow.

After breakfast, Connor hurried upstairs to get dressed while I helped Aunt Jackie finish up the dishes. Then we all trooped outside to the car. Connor took the front seat while Bri and I got into the back. As I buckled my seat belt, I couldn't help thinking about what had happened yesterday. Sitting here in this very seat then suddenly falling into a vision of some great, horrible darkness.

I tried to shake off this image and stare out the window as Aunt Jackie guided the car down the winding road to Ballymore. The sky overhead was bright blue, but I could see dark clouds on the horizon.

Aunt Jackie found a parking spot close to Main Street. After we piled out of the car, she handed each of us five euros.

"For sweets," she said, ruffling Bri's hair affectionately. "I'm going to run a few errands. Meet me at the playground in half an hour, okay?"

"Okay!" we chorused.

After Aunt Jackie headed off toward the pharmacy, Connor, Bri, and I made a beeline for Shay's Sweets. When we walked out five minutes later, all three of us were clutching paper bags stuffed with strawberry laces, jellies, and pear drops.

I cast a sideways glance at Connor as we strolled down Main Street. This was my chance to tell him what had happened.

"So, Granny told us a story last night," I began, poking around my bag in search of another pear drop. "She said it was Dad's favorite when he was little. It was about the Fae . . . but it was pretty intense."

Connor snorted. "Of course it was. She's always intense about those stories." He gave me a small smile. "Your dad is, too. Sometimes I think he really believes in all that stuff."

The pear drop stuck in my throat, and I coughed a little. "Yeah, me, too."

Connor fished another strawberry string from his bag. "My mom says he never grew out of it. Not in a bad way," he added hastily, noticing my expression. "She loves that about him. That he believed in . . ." Connor waved his strawberry string in the air. "Magic, or whatever."

I watched as he popped it into his mouth.

On his other side, Bri was pecking at her own bag with her raven. She didn't look at me, but I could tell she was listening intently.

I had been so ready to tell Connor about the Bow. About her comb, and the curse, and everything that had happened since we'd arrived yesterday. But the dismissive way he'd said *Magic, or whatever* . . . if my enthusiasm was an inflated balloon, Connor had just popped it.

He would think I was nuts if I told him what I saw on Coffin Rock. I felt the fairy stone hanging from my neck and imagined

Connor's face if I tried to explain that I'd looked through the hole and seen the Bow. He was way too nice to make fun of me. He would probably look surprised, then worried . . . worse, he might look like he felt sorry for me.

As we drew closer to the playground, I heard a dog barking. Up ahead, I spotted two boys and a girl talking to an elderly man.

Not talking. Taunting.

"Ugh." Connor slowed his pace slightly when he noticed them. "Rob Lalor's such a jerk. And Jude's not much better."

But my eyes were on the girl because I recognized her now. I'd met Rose on the sailing course last summer, and we'd actually become pretty good friends. I caught her eye and waved, but she ignored me.

I ducked my head, feeling a blush creep up my neck. I tried to tell myself she hadn't seen me, or maybe hadn't recognized me. But something about the way her posture stiffened told me she knew I'd seen her, and she wasn't happy about it.

Rob was jumping up and down, trying to grab a low-hanging branch that stretched out over the pavement while his enormous black dog barked aggressively. The tree itself was on the old man's property, and he clearly wasn't happy about Rob's antics. As Connor, Bri, and I walked closer, I recognized the man as Jimmy Jo. He was a loner, the kind of guy everyone in town knew and tended to steer clear of because he liked to rant to anyone who paid him the least bit of attention.

I slowed down, watching Jimmy more carefully. Every time Rob leaped up and grabbed the branch, the old man would cry out and clutch his stomach . . . almost as if Rob touching the tree were causing him physical pain. He lurched forward every time Rob landed, but then the dog would let out a ferocious bark, baring his teeth, and Jimmy would retract his steps.

Jimmy's behavior was alarming sometimes, but he didn't deserve this. Jude was openly laughing, and Rob's grin was wide as he leaped up and grabbed the branch yet again.

Next to Jude, Rose watched with an impassive expression. She wasn't laughing, at least. But she also wasn't doing anything to stop Rob.

Of course, neither was I.

"Should we do something?" I muttered to Connor. Bri had gone very still, staring hard at Rob. With a start, I realized her raven appeared to be staring at him, too.

Connor grimaced. "I guess we could find an adult . . . but no one's gonna yell at Rob. They all know who his dad is."

Rob *Lalor*. I suddenly remembered my conversation with Granny in the kitchen yesterday. "He's the one building that microplastic factory!"

"Yeah." Connor shook his head. "Don't get Sean started on that. He'll talk your ear off about how bad it'll be for the environment. He's obsessed."

"Really?" I hadn't seen Sean in a while, but the only thing I remembered him obsessing over was video games and comics. "He's right, though."

"Well, obviously."

Connor fell silent as Jimmy shouted loud enough for us to hear.

"Don't you hurt that tree, sonny!"

"Or what?" Rob sneered, brushing off his hands on his jeans.

"Or the shadow, creatures will come!" Jimmy hollered. "You'll see!"

Jude howled with laughter as Rob smirked. "Well, I'll just have to risk it."

He leaped up again, grabbing the branch—and this time, it broke off with a sickening *snap*. Jimmy cried out in agony, doubling over as Rob waved the broken branch at his dog. It looked like the beast from a dark fairy tale, midnight black and muscular, with pointy ears and rows of sharp teeth.

Rob reeled back to throw the branch, and I knew what would happen the moment before it did.

The dog lunged for the branch, jaws open wide. But Jimmy leaped forward, too, reaching for it. His fingers closed around the branch a half-second before the dog's teeth clamped down on his wrist.

"Aahhhhhhhhh!"

I ran forward, Connor right at my side. But as I moved to the awful scene—Jimmy clutching his arm, his shirtsleeve stained with blood; the snarling, beast-like dog; Rob and Jude's cruel laughter; Rose just *standing* there—something started to happen.

My vision blurred, and the world went dark around the edges until all I could see was Rob Lalor. I was gripped with the same all-consuming terror I'd felt in the car yesterday. The fear of the void.

"Squawk! Squawk! Squawk!"

The sound of Bri's hoarse, angry screeches brought me back to the present. Turning, I was shocked to see her face was bright red with rage, tears streaming down her cheeks as she waved her raven puppet and squawked furiously.

Rob and Jude looked at Bri then at one another. Then they doubled over, laughing harder than ever. Rose took a step back, and for a moment, I thought she was going to simply run away. Jimmy's howls finally stopped, but he cradled his bloody arm as he watched Bri with a curious expression.

"Look who it is!" Rob said when he caught his breath. "Kathleen's hippie grandkids coming to rescue the weird old man! Why don't you all go hug a tree together? Are you gonna use some of your granny's mumbo jumbo on us?" He kicked the branch resting on the ground. Next to him, the dog snarled.

"Rose," I said, my voice cracking. "Please tell them to stop this."

A flicker of guilt passed over Rose's face. Then she let out a huffy sigh.

"What makes you think you can just order me around?"

The harshness of her tone hit me like a slap across the face. I stared at her, stupefied. Rose and I were friends last summer. What happened to her?

Blood rushed to my cheeks as Jimmy stepped forward, ignoring the dog's warning growl. His dark, glittering eyes were fixed on Rob.

"No coming back once the darkness takes hold of you, sonny," he hissed. "Ignis is coming. The shadow creatures too."

Ignis. My entire body flashed hot then ice-cold.

"You've lost it, old man," Rob jeered. He snapped his fingers, and his dog grabbed the branch in his jaws and stood. "Let's go."

Rob and Jude walked off, the dog trotting at Rob's side. Rose trailed behind them, not meeting my gaze even once.

Connor let out a sigh. "Good riddance," he muttered. "You okay, Jimmy?"

Jimmy didn't respond. His eyes were locked onto Bri. She was still trembling with anger, but she met his gaze unblinkingly.

"So, you're the one," he told her softly.

My pulse quickened. "What do you mean?"

He didn't take his eyes off Bri when he responded. "I heard about your da. Went looking for it, he did. You will, too. But be careful—the curse is strong."

Goosebumps broke out all over my arms. I couldn't even speak as Jimmy turned and trundled up the path to his house. He slammed the door behind him, but his words rang over and over in my mind. *Ignis is coming. Your da went looking for it. The curse is strong.*

"Rob's a jerk, but he's right about one thing," Connor said. When I stared at him blankly, he added as if it were obvious, "Jimmy's lost it."

My mouth opened and closed. I had no idea what to say to that.

"And he had no right talking about your dad like that," Connor said, putting his arm around Bri. "I'm sorry, guys. Don't listen to him, okay? Jimmy's always talking Fae nonsense. No one's crazy enough to believe it."

I gazed at my cousin's earnest expression, and suddenly I knew there was no way I could tell him about the Bow. He would think my sadness over Dad was making me lose it, just like Jimmy Jo.

"You're right," I said softly. "You okay, Bri?"

Wiping her eyes, she nodded and offered a weak smile.

As we continued toward the playground, Connor changed the subject back to the Halloween party. But my mind was on everything Jimmy had said. *The curse is strong.*

I had to return the Bow's comb before things got worse. And I had to do it alone.

- SIX -

The Stone
of Destiny

AUNT JACKIE PICKED us up moments before the storm clouds arrived, unleashing heavy drops of ice-cold rain that splashed against the windows. I waved goodbye to her and Connor as Bri and I scrambled out of the car and sprinted for the door.

The house was quiet. Too quiet.

I frowned as I unzipped my coat and kicked off my shoes. There was always noise in this house: the clanking of pots, the chatter of the radio, the crackle of flames in the fireplace. But now it was silent as a tomb.

Bri looked at me nervously, and I tried to smile.

"Maybe Granny went out for a walk," I said then immediately realized how ridiculous that would be, considering it was pouring rain outside. "I'll check upstairs, okay?"

She nodded, and I took the stairs two at a time. At the end of the hall, Granny's bedroom door was cracked open an inch. I pushed it open gingerly.

"Granny?"

At first, I thought she hadn't made her bed. Then I noticed the lump under the tangled blankets and my heart skipped a beat. I hurried closer until I could see her face poking out from under the quilt. She was horribly pale, and for one heart-stopping moment, I thought she wasn't breathing.

Then she exhaled faintly, and I went weak with relief. But that feeling didn't last long. Something was definitely wrong. Her complexion was sallow and the collar of her nightdress was soaked with sweat. She mumbled something indistinct and rolled over on her back.

"Granny?" I whispered. Then I raised my voice. "Granny, wake up!"

"Mmmph," she muttered, her head lolling from side to side. Her eyelashes started fluttering, and I glimpsed the whites of her eyes. "Give it back . . . she can help . . . the curse . . . *Michael!*"

I took a step back, alarmed. She was having a nightmare about Dad. But maybe it was more than just a nightmare. *Give it back . . .* The realization caused my stomach to drop like I'd just gone over the peak of a roller coaster.

Was she talking about the Bow's comb?

Hands trembling, I picked up the phone on Granny's nightstand and dialed. To my relief, Uncle Pat picked up before the second ring.

"It's Cara," I said quickly. "Granny's sick. Really sick. I don't know what to do."

Uncle Pat's voice was calm and reassuring. "I'll call Dr. O'Neill, and Aunt Jackie will come right over. Stay with Granny until then, okay?"

"Okay."

"It's probably just the flu," Uncle Pat said. "It's that time of year. Don't worry, Cara."

"Thanks," I whispered, then hung up the phone. But as I looked at Granny's pale, sweaty face, I knew this was no flu.

It was the curse.

∽

Aunt Jackie showed up fifteen minutes later, quickly followed by Dr. O'Neill. I left them in Granny's room and hurried down the hall. I couldn't bear seeing Granny look so ill.

When I entered my room, I found Bri sitting cross-legged on her bed. She was sketching furiously in her art pad, raven puppet at her side.

"The doctor's here," I told her, raising my voice over the sound of the rain against the window. "Granny's going to be fine. Probably just the flu."

I didn't even believe my own words, so I couldn't blame Bri when she glanced up long enough to give me a look that clearly said, *Oh, please.* Even her raven seemed to be glaring at me.

"Can I see your drawing?" I asked, moving closer. The moment the question left my lips, I wanted to take it back. Her sketch of the Bow had given me the creeps.

Bri shrugged one shoulder, her black pencil still flying over the page. I leaned over her bed to get a look at the paper.

It was a mountain, all jagged and looming high over the tiny row of trees around the base. As I looked closer, I could just make out what looked like steps along the left side. I opened my mouth, ready to compliment Bri on her skills . . . then I realized what I was looking at.

This wasn't just any mountain. It was Carrauntoohil.

I swallowed, my mouth suddenly bone-dry.

Bri continued sketching, shading in more details on the mountain, adding a low-hanging cloud.

My sister had drawn the Bow less than an hour before we'd seen her. Now she was drawing the mountain where Dad was lost . . . or worse.

Was it possible Bri knew something about Dad's disappearance? Where he was on the path, whether he was injured, or . . .

My pulse began to race, and I realized my vision was going dark. It was happening again.

I stumbled out of the room and down the hall into Granny's study. I could see the armchair, the shelves stuffed with books, the desk covered in papers, the framed photos in clusters on the fireplace mantle . . . but only through a veil of darkness, as if I were half in this world, half in the void.

You catch a little bit of your power. Dad's voice drifted in the air, barely above a whisper but crystal clear, as if he were standing right there with me. *And you tune in to it.*

"Tune into it," I mumbled, struggling not to panic, to focus on the study. The darkness lifted slightly, the study coming more into view—and then a glimmer of light on the desk caught my eye.

A low humming sound filled my ears as I approached the desk. I could sense Dad right next to me. It felt as if I would see him smiling down at me encouragingly if I looked up . . . but I knew if I did, I wouldn't see him, and the disappointment would be crushing. So, I kept my eyes on the glimmer.

I moved a stack of folders and a few stray papers aside and found myself staring at a small slip of paper with a few words scrawled on it. I recognized Dad's handwriting instantly and felt an odd twang in my chest, like a guitar string had just been plucked. I picked it up and read it once, twice, three times.

Door on Carrauntoohil . . . Stone of Destiny??

"Dad," I whispered, squeezing the note tightly. "Is this why you went on that hike?"

I knew the answer was yes, even though Dad wasn't here to confirm it. Sucking in a deep breath, I tried to think rationally. Dad's decision to go on a hike had been rather sudden. And the timing was strange, considering Mom had just had a baby. *It's urgent,* he'd said.

Why had finding the stone been *urgent*? Why did Dad need it so desperately?

And suddenly, I remembered the words from Granny's book.

There is one whom the Fae fear, one Druid who uses dark magic to create thought enchantments that increase the darkness, who manipulates the earthly realm. He forged an alliance with the Formors and is committed to helping them find and destroy the Stone of Destiny.

He is called Ignis.

My pulse began to race again as I heard Jimmy Jo's warning to Rob Lalor. *Ignis is coming!* Maybe Dad wasn't just trying to find the stone. Maybe he was trying to find it *first*. Before Ignis found it and destroyed it.

I shoved Dad's note into my pocket. The darkness had faded, but this time I wasn't relieved. I was getting better at "tuning in," and I wanted another try at it. I wanted to connect with Dad again. But I couldn't control when those moments came, and it was beyond frustrating.

Outside, the rain was finally starting to let up. I probably had a few more hours of daylight left, and Aunt Jackie was busy tending to Granny. If I was going to return the comb to the Bow, this might be my best chance.

I leaned against the desk and pulled out my phone. I did a quick search for local tide times and groaned. It was high tide now. Coffin Rock would be surrounded by water.

Sighing, I closed the browser and started to leave the study. I passed the mantel—then stopped, turning to look at the photos.

Something had caught my eye, but what? I moved closer, my gaze locking in on a wooden frame. Along the top was an engraving:

BALLYMORE GROVE OF DRUIDS

I reached out and picked it up, inspecting the photo. Granny was much younger, but her long plait and twinkling eyes were unmistakable. She stood with a woman and a man in a field surrounded by standing stones. I didn't recognize the woman at all, but there was something familiar about the man. His dark hair was scraped back into a tight ponytail, and while the two women were smiling at the camera, the man was looking at Granny, his lips twisted into a sneer.

Recognition dawned, and my skin crawled. "Frank the fisherman," I whispered.

He'd been here yesterday, yelling at Granny about a curse. And Granny had lied to me, making it sound like he was just worked up about Brian Lalor's microplastic factory.

My phone buzzed, making me jump. I glanced at the screen and saw a text from Connor.

Granny ok?

Setting the framed photo back on the mantel, I typed out a response. *Not sure. Doc is here.*

He replied with a thumbs-up emoji and then: *u ok?*

Automatically, I typed *yes*. But my thumb hovered over *Send* as I looked at the photo of Granny and Frank.

I wasn't okay. It suddenly felt as though everyone I loved and trusted was keeping secrets from me. Everyone except Connor.

I couldn't do this alone. I had to tell him everything. I had to convince him I hadn't lost it like Jimmy Jo—and that even Jimmy Jo might not be as crazy as Connor thought.

Now that I'd found actual evidence to show Connor, maybe I could prove to him that this was all real.

Not really, I typed. *Can I come over?*

His response was immediate. *Sure. I'm in the base.*

I shoved my phone in my pocket, snatched the photo of Granny and Frank off the mantel, and marched out the door.

- SEVEN -

The Otherworld

A T THE FRONT DOOR, I pulled on my jacket and wellies. The worst of the storm had passed, but I could make out a light drizzle outside through the fogged-up window. I reached for the door handle, and—

THUD. THUD. THUD.

I yanked my hand away, startled, and stared at the door.

"Who is it?" I called weakly. No response. Frowning, I stepped forward and pulled the door open.

No one.

I stuck my head out and looked around the porch. Unease settled over me as I stepped outside and began to close the door. But then I spotted Bri huddled at the top of the staircase, clutching her raven.

"Did you hear that?" I asked her. "Those knocks?"

She stared at me blankly. I waited a moment then let out a sigh of frustration and pulled the door closed firmly behind me. It was only then that I remembered what Dad had told us about the Bow. *Others have said they heard her cries just before a death in the family . . . or that she knocked on their door three times.*

My skin crawled, and I stared around the yard, half-expecting to see a hooded figure lurking in the woods. I saw no one, but it didn't matter. I'd heard her knock.

The Bow had given me a warning. Time was running out.

I ran all the way to Connor's place, my boots squelching as the mud did its best to slow me down. By the time his house came into view, the drizzle had lightened to a fine mist. A "soft" day, that was what Dad would call this. My hair clung to my forehead in damp strands, and I pushed my hood back as I hurried around the back of the house.

A few years ago, Uncle Pat had built a tree house for Connor. It was hard to see until you were standing right under it, and Connor and I often used it to escape our more annoying cousins during family visits. We called it the base.

I made my way to the giant oak tree and began to climb up the planks nailed into the trunk. "Hey," I said, pulling myself up. "So, listen, I know this . . . oh."

My stomach sank as I realized Connor wasn't alone. His best friend, Sean, sat next to him, jet-black hair sticking up in all directions. They were surrounded by open bags of crisps, both staring intently at Sean's phone as they munched. Connor was wearing his glasses, which surprised me—he hardly ever bothered with them these days.

"Hey, Cara!" Sean said.

"Hey." I tried to hide my disappointment as I settled on the floor opposite them. Normally, I'd be happy to see Sean. He was nice, and he could be really funny sometimes. Sean was Vietnamese—his mom and dad had adopted him when he was just a baby. They owned a bakery in Ballymore, which meant hanging out with him often came with free scones.

But I needed to tell Connor about the Bow, the curse, Ignis . . . not exactly a conversation I wanted to have in front of anyone else.

"Sorry about your gran," Sean said. "It must've been scary to come home and find her so sick."

I pictured Granny's pale face and fluttering lashes as she'd moaned in her sleep. "Yeah, it was. I'm worried about her."

"She was fine this morning," Connor said, frowning. "If she's coming down with the flu, I'm sure Dr. O'Neill will—"

"It's not the flu." I took a deep breath. *You have proof,* I reminded myself. *You haven't lost it. You can make them understand.* "I think it's . . . I think it's a curse."

Connor and Sean both stared at me for several long seconds.

"Sorry, what?" Connor said at last.

I shrugged off my jacket then pulled the note and the picture frame from the pockets. "I found these in Granny's study," I said, speaking slowly and carefully. "This is a note from my dad. Now I know why he went on that hike when it was so treacherous. He was looking for a door on Carrauntoohil where the Stone of Destiny is hidden."

Connor wiped the crisp crumbs from his hands before taking the note. He scanned it then looked up at me.

I saw a flash of pity in his eyes and chose to ignore it.

"And this is a photo of Granny and Frank the fisherman," I continued, holding up the frame. *"Ballymore Grove of the Druids.* Granny has a journal all about Druid magic—I read it. She wrote that Druids work with sparkle, but there is one Druid the Fae fear because he uses dark magic. He wants to destroy the Stone of Destiny. His name is Ignis."

I set the picture frame down between us. Sean hadn't so much as blinked since I started talking. Connor watched me carefully, chewing his lower lip.

"Ignis," he repeated, brow furrowing. "Wait—didn't Jimmy Jo say something about Ignis?"

I nodded, my stomach tightening. "He did, yeah. But I—I don't think he's lost it, Connor. I think Granny and Frank and Dad all believe in this stuff because they know it's real." I lifted my chin defiantly. "And I know it's real, too. Last night, I . . . I saw the Bow."

Wind howled through the trees outside, and a cold gust of air through the window made me wish I hadn't taken off my coat. A half-empty crisp bag went skittering across the wooden floor, stopping only when it hit the wall. Neither Connor nor Sean moved to retrieve it.

"The Bow," Connor said slowly.

I explained everything. Bri's eerie drawing, that awful wailing sound, the way Bri had walked toward Coffin Rock as if in a trance.

"And before you say it might have been some sort of animal," I added, fishing out the cord from under my shirt, "I know it was the Bow because I saw her . . . through this." I held up the stone.

Connor and Sean looked at it.

"It's a fairy stone," I said. "It belonged to my dad. I found it in the woodshed. And when I looked through it, I saw the Bow, clear as day." I let the stone fall back to my chest. "I pulled Bri away and took her home. But then this morning, she showed me a comb—the Bow's comb! Bri found it and she was trying to return it, and I stopped her. So now I need to return it so she'll help us stop the curse and—"

"Whoa, hang on," Sean interrupted. "Are my processors broken, or are you talking about *fairies*?" He pretended to adjust the processors that sat like two magnets on either side of his head, both connected to the cochlear implants in his ears.

I ignored the joke and turned to Connor. "Don't you get it? My dad was trying to get the Stone of Destiny before Ignis, and Ignis cursed our family! That's why Dad's missing—not to mention your cattle's blackleg, and Bri not being able to talk, and now Granny getting so sick out of nowhere. It's the curse! I heard Granny talking in her sleep. She said, *Give it back . . . she can help . . . the curse . . . Michael.* Granny *knows* all of this is real. She knows that if I return the Bow's comb, she can help me find a way into the fairy realm and save my dad!"

My voice had risen to a fever pitch. I fell silent, my cheeks flushing hot with embarrassment as I looked pleadingly at Connor. "Look, I know it sounds weird, but you have to believe me."

Connor looked back down at Dad's note. An awkward silence fell, and after a moment, Sean cleared his throat.

"Is this all a Halloween gag?" he asked, grinning at me. "A curse, evil fairies, *wooOOOooo . . .*" He waggled his fingers in a spooky gesture and made his voice all wobbly. When I didn't laugh, his smile vanished and he dropped his hands to his sides. "Okay, guess not."

"This is definitely your dad's handwriting?" Connor asked, holding up the note.

I nodded firmly. "Absolutely. And Granny wrote about Ignis in her journal, Connor. I know you think Jimmy Jo's weird, but you don't think she's lost it, too, do you? Or my dad? I even overheard Granny talking to your mom about the curse yesterday! And Frank, too!"

"Frank?" Connor said, glancing back at the photo. "When?"

"He was at Granny's house when we got there yesterday," I told him. "He was ranting and raving at her, and he said something about a curse. I asked Granny about it, but she said he was upset about Brian Lalor's microplastic factory."

Sean perked up at that. "Oh yeah? Maybe I should tell him about my protest." He caught my blank look and added, "I'm organizing a protest to stop them from building that factory. It would be terrible for the environment."

"It would," I agreed. "But I heard Frank yelling about a *curse*, not a factory. Granny lied to me." I turned back to Connor. "Either all the grown-ups we know have lost it or . . . or it's all real."

"I'm not—*ahh!*" Connor yelped, pointing behind me.

I leaped up and turned around, my heart skipping a beat when I saw the black creature with beady yellow eyes poking up through the tree house entrance.

"Squawk?"

My shoulders slumped in relief, and I rolled my eyes. "Bri, stop trying to scare us."

A pale hand appeared next to the raven, and my sister pulled herself up into the tree house. Her doleful gaze moved from Connor to Sean, and she smiled a little shyly.

Sean clasped his hand to his heart in mock terror. "What a great prank! You scared us half to death, Bri!" he exclaimed.

Bri giggled, clearly pleased.

"Who's your friend?"

Bri shuffled over and sat next to Sean, holding up the raven. "Squawk."

"Squawk?" Sean repeated. "No offense, but that's not the best name for a raven. I bet we can come up with a better one."

The raven puppet nodded vigorously. Bri gazed at Sean as he began suggesting names, her eyes lighting up.

I moved closer to Connor and lowered my voice. "I know you think I'm losing it, but—"

"No, I don't," Connor said. He looked at me sympathetically. "It does feel like our family is cursed right now. Everything's going wrong. And this . . ." He waved Dad's note again. "I mean, I get what you're saying. Granny, Uncle Michael, my mom . . . they aren't telling us something."

"And Bri," I whispered. "Granny asked me when exactly she stopped talking, and she made me realize it was *before* we got that call from Kerry. *Before* we even knew Dad was missing. I think . . ." I paused, watching as Sean ruffled the raven's feathers, causing Bri to giggle again. "I think Bri knew something bad had happened to him before we did. She drew a picture of Carrauntoohil. She drew the Bow before we saw her, Connor."

"Mom thinks Bri not talking is just her way of . . ." Connor paused, glancing at me nervously. "Well, of grieving," he finished, a note of apology in his voice. "Maybe that's what the pictures are about?"

I sighed, frustrated. "You still don't believe me."

"I do," Connor said hastily. "I believe you're right about Granny and our parents not telling us something. But, Cara, that doesn't mean *fairies* are real."

I sat back on my heels, feeling deflated. I could see Connor's point. Part of me couldn't help but wonder if maybe my grief was getting the better of me, too. Maybe I only saw the Bow when I looked through the fairy stone because I'd wanted to. Because I wanted to believe Dad was still alive.

"Besides," Connor added. "Aren't fairies supposed to be cute little beings with wings who grant wishes? This stuff you're talking about all sounds really dark."

I rolled my eyes. "Tell that to Granny and my dad. The stories they told me and Bri were always super dark."

"Um, guys?" Sean said.

Connor and I turned to see him holding the Ballymore Grove of Druids photo. Next to him, Bri pecked at the frame with her raven.

"What?" I asked.

Sean squinted at the photo. "This woman who's with Frank and your gran . . . I know her."

"You do?"

"Yeah!" Sean looked up. "Connor, you know her, too. It's Miss F."

He held the photo out, and Connor took it. "Oh, yeah, I think you're right!"

"Who is she?" I asked eagerly.

"Our old music teacher," Sean explained. "She retired a few years ago. She's a lot younger in this picture, but that's her." He tapped the photo. "See that silver ring with the white stone? She always wore that. I remember it."

I studied the ring glinting on her hand. "Did she ever mention anything about Druids or the Fae?"

"Not that I remember."

"Does she live around here?" I asked, already getting to my feet. "Maybe she can tell us—" I paused, glancing at Connor. "Whatever it is Granny isn't telling us."

Sean's face fell. "Actually, she's in the hospital. She got in this terrible car accident a few months ago. My mom said she suffered a head injury. Pretty sure she can't talk to anyone."

My stomach clenched tight. *The curse,* I thought, but I didn't say it out loud. Instead, I took a deep breath and looked from Sean to Connor. "Then I think we should go talk to Jimmy Jo."

"We?" Sean yelped at the same time as Connor said, "Jimmy Jo?"

"Yes." I crossed my arms. "He might be the only grown-up willing to tell us whatever this secret is that they're all keeping from us. Name one good reason we shouldn't at least ask him about it."

Connor was silent for a moment. Then he shrugged. "You win," he said with a smile. "Let's talk to him."

"Squawk?"

We looked at Bri, who was gesturing to the window with her puppet. I realized with a start that the sky was already growing dark.

"Tomorrow morning?" I asked, turning back to Connor.

He nodded. "Tomorrow morning."

"Why not?" Sean said, smiling at me. "I'm in."

I returned the smile, although inside, my nerves were churning. Connor had made a good point. Just because the grown-ups were keeping a secret didn't mean the secret was that the Fae were real. And I didn't much care for the idea that my feelings were making me hallucinate.

But more importantly, I needed to believe that Dad was alive. That he hadn't simply had an accident during a hike. That there was some way I could save him.

And Jimmy Jo might be the only person who could give me the answers I needed.

- EIGHT -

Capturing
a Fae

AUNT JACKIE WAS HEATING up leftover soup when Bri and I entered the kitchen. The warm, spicy aroma was comforting, but Granny's absence was hard to ignore.

"Dr. O'Neill assured me she'll be fine in no time," Aunt Jackie said as she ladled the soup into bowls. "She just needs rest and plenty of fluids."

I wanted to believe her. But I could see the worry in Aunt Jackie's eyes, even as she tried to smile. And I knew, without a doubt, that I was right. Granny didn't have the flu.

It was the curse.

Bri and I ate in silence while Aunt Jackie cleaned up the kitchen. When she finished, she pulled up a chair between us.

"Have you girls been making good use of the gifts Granny gave you?"

Bri nodded enthusiastically.

I pictured the beautiful journal with the silver Irish knot on the cover and felt a pang of guilt. "Bri's been using her art pad a lot, but I haven't written in my journal yet," I admitted.

"You should give it a try!" Aunt Jackie placed her hand on mine, holding my gaze. "Sometimes when things are uncertain, it's natural for our minds to try and seek answers. Writing might help you with that."

I swallowed hard and nodded. "I will."

"And if you have anything you want to talk to me about, I'm always here for you."

"I know."

I had plenty I wanted to talk about. But I'd already tried talking to Aunt Jackie and Granny about the curse. Besides, I knew what she meant. She was talking about Dad. About the possibility that he might be . . .

Ducking my head, I focused on finishing my soup. I wouldn't allow myself to think that way. I couldn't.

"Cara, what's that?"

I glanced up and saw Aunt Jackie pointing at the cord around my neck. I felt for it and pulled the stone out from under my shirt.

"Oh, I found this in the woodshed," I said uncomfortably. "I thought it was . . ." I paused. *Pretty* wasn't exactly the right word, but I didn't want her to know the real reason I'd kept it. "I guess I just like it. It helps me feel more—"

"Grounded?" Aunt Jackie suggested. When I frowned, she continued. "Stones are very good at connecting us to the earth's energy, as well as our inner energies. Try this."

She took hold of my wrists and placed my right hand on the fairy stone and my left hand on my stomach.

"Now close your eyes and take a long, deep breath through your nose . . ."

I obeyed, shifting a little in my chair.

"Breathing in peace and calm, one, two, three, four . . . and breathing out worry and fear, one, two, three, four, five, six . . ."

I felt silly at first. But listening to Aunt Jackie's soothing voice, I started to relax, and soon the knot in my stomach had loosened. She counted through the exercise three more times then patted my arm.

"See? If you ever feel anxious, taking a few seconds to focus on your breathing can really help."

"It did," I said, picking up my spoon again. "Thanks, Aunt Jackie."

After dinner, I went to check on Granny. She was sound asleep, and I was relieved to see some of the color had returned to her cheeks. But when I kissed her on the cheek, her skin was cool and clammy despite the layers of blankets keeping her warm.

In the crate near her bed, Hugo the hedgehog was curled up into a tight, spiky ball. I couldn't help wondering whether he was hibernating or the curse had spread to him, too.

Aunt Jackie made up a bed on the sofa downstairs. Part of me wanted to tell her she could go home, that Bri and I would be just fine. But another part of me was relieved she would be here. The curse had struck Granny, and I was terrified of what might happen next.

Bri was already in bed with the lights off by the time I finished brushing my teeth. I climbed into my own bed, but I wasn't sleepy at all. So, I switched my flashlight on, grabbed the journal and pen Granny had given me, and began to write.

I wrote about everything: Ignis and the curse, the Bow and the comb, my fears about Bri and her drawings, and how much I missed Dad and Mom. By the time I finished, my hand was cramping, but I did feel a little bit lighter. I closed the journal and set it on my night table.

Something slipped off the table and hit the floor with a soft *thump*. Leaning over the side of my bed, I groped around until my fingers closed around a book.

I sat up and shone the flashlight onto the cover. *THE STONE OF DESTINY.*

My heart began to pound. Had I taken this from Granny's study? No, I definitely had not. I remembered putting this book down once I found Granny's journal. So why was it here on my night table?

I glanced over at the blanket-covered lump that was my sister. Then I leaned back against my pillows and flipped through the book. Something caught my eye—not a word but an image—and I hastily flicked back page by page until I found it.

The drawing was labeled *The Stone of Destiny*. It was a fairly simple sketch, but something about the shape of it was intensely familiar. After a few seconds, realization dawned and I gasped.

Shoving my blankets off, I slipped out of bed and tiptoed across the room. Bri's art pad lay on her night table, and I opened it as quietly as possible, turning page after page until I found her drawing of Carrauntoohil. I propped the book up against the lamp, then rotated Bri's art pad sideways. My throat tightened, and I drew a shallow breath.

They were identical. Bri hadn't drawn the mountain. She'd drawn the Stone of Destiny.

A mix of dread and wonder flooded through me. I closed Bri's art pad and took the book back to bed. I gazed at the drawing until my eyelids started to droop. Sighing, I flipped the page, intending to check for any other drawings before closing the book and going to sleep. But when I saw the other side of the page, I froze.

Cramped, slightly smudged print filled the margins. I recognized it right away—the words and the handwriting.

Dad had written in this book. The words were from a poem by Rudyard Kipling I'd heard him quote many times.

Something hidden. Go and find it. Go and look behind the Ranges.

Something lost behind the Ranges. Lost and waiting for you. Go!

Adrenaline thrummed through me, all thoughts of sleep forgotten. If I'd had any doubts before, they were gone. Dad had gone looking for the Stone of Destiny. He had gone looking for the Otherworld.

He was still there. And I had to figure out a way to find him and bring him home.

NINE

The Explorer

BUZZ-BUZZ. I blinked blearily, the room coming into focus. My eyelids scratched like sandpaper. I rolled onto my side as a dull throbbing started in my temples. I had lain awake for hours last night, and now I felt as if I'd barely slept at all.

Buzz-buzz.

I glanced at the night table and saw my phone's screen lit up with a text. With a groan, I picked up the phone and squinted to read the messages.

Sean and I will be there in 5 mins.
Bringing bikes for you and Bri.

Connor. I sat up straight, my eyes going to Bri's empty bed. We'd made plans to bike over to Jimmy Jo's this morning, and I'd slept in.

I threw on jeans and a sweater, brushed my teeth, and raced downstairs. Through the window, I could see Connor, Sean, and Bri talking. Four bikes were propped up against the metal gate.

"Cara?" Aunt Jackie appeared in the kitchen doorway as I shoved my feet into my boots. "I was about to make some oatmeal. What's the rush?"

"No rush," I said quickly. "We, um . . . we're going to get something from Sean's parents' bakery in Ballymore. How's Granny this morning?"

"Better," Aunt Jackie said with a smile. "She even sat up and had a bit of tea earlier this morning."

Relief swept through me. "Oh, good. We'll be back for lunch, okay?"

"Have a nice time!" She disappeared back into the kitchen, and I hurried outside.

Connor spotted me heading down the path. "There you are! I was just about to text you again."

"Sorry, I slept late," I said, glancing at Bri.

She didn't meet my gaze, keeping her focus on her raven instead. Had she put that book on my night table? I was longing to ask her, but I knew she wouldn't answer. As much as I loved my sister, I couldn't help feeling a wave of frustration at her stubborn silence.

"Hungry?" Sean said, holding out a paper bag. The wind had whipped his hair around, making it stick up in the back even more than usual. "I brought a few extra scones."

"Thanks," I said, taking a raspberry scone from the bag. "We'd better get going. It's a pretty long bike ride to Jimmy's."

I ate the scone in three giant bites as the others climbed onto their bikes. Then I grabbed the handlebars of the last bike and swung my leg over the seat.

"Let's go!"

A few smoke-gray clouds drifted across the otherwise blue sky, and the sun would peek out from behind them every few minutes. As anxious as I was about talking to Jimmy Jo, I couldn't help enjoying the ride down the country road, listening to the shallow water lapping against the ragged, rocky shore.

After a few minutes, I noticed a robin flitting from tree to tree, staying just ahead of us. I wondered whether it was the robin I'd spotted in the fairy tree . . . the one that had whispered my name. I put on a burst of speed, trying to get closer, but the robin kept darting ahead, and I couldn't quite tell.

"There it is!" Sean called up ahead, slowing down. I began to brake, looking at the overgrown shrubs wrapped tightly against a wrought-iron gate. The four of us came to a stop in front of Jimmy Jo's cottage. I glanced around for the robin, but it was nowhere to be seen.

The cottage was made of dark stone, and the windows were oddly tiny. An old red tractor with a front wheel half off sat in the dead grass out front, tilting to the side. We propped up our bikes against the gate.

"What's with all the garden gnomes?" Connor asked.

I wrinkled my nose, my eyes scanning the yard. Dozens of the little statues were scattered around the property, some peeping up behind the scraggly bushes along the house, others sitting stoutly out in the grass. Most had too-wide eyes and creepy smiles. A few were missing parts: a leg, an arm, even a nose. One had a black hole where its left eye should have been.

"They're kind of freaky," I said, and Connor nodded in agreement.

"It looks dark in the windows," Sean said. "Maybe he's not home."

"Squawk!" Bri pointed with her raven at the roof of the cottage. I looked up and saw a thin wisp of smoke snaking out of the chimney, barely visible against the backdrop of trees.

"Well, guess I was wrong about that!" Sean grinned at the puppet. "Good eye, Corwin."

Bri ducked her head, her expression pleased.

"Corwin?" I asked, undoing the latch on the gate. It swung open with a high-pitched *creak*.

"That's the name we picked for her raven," Sean informed me. "It suits him, doesn't it?"

"Raven Corwin, come to me,
Hear my call, beside me be . . ."

I heard Granny's voice as clearly as if she was standing beside me. "Corwin, as in the raven that helped Lugh fight Balor?"

Sean blinked. "Helped who fight what?"

I sighed. "Never mind."

The four of us trudged up the dirt path to the cottage's front door. I tried not to look down at the garden gnomes, but I imagined their eyes following me and suppressed a shiver.

The front door was in bad need of a paint job. I thought it had been black once, but years of wear and tear had left it more of a mottled gray, all peeling and splintered. The tarnished door knocker was shaped like a fox.

Steeling myself, I reached up and pulled it back then rapped it firmly and loudly against the door.

The first knock set off a frenzied barking inside that caused me to leap away in alarm. I bumped into Sean, who lost his balance on the edge of the porch stoop.

"Ah!" he exclaimed, his arms windmilling comically as he teetered backward. I reached out and grabbed the front of his shirt, pulling him toward me. For a moment, we were almost nose-to-nose, and then I backed up hastily.

"Sorry about that!" I said, annoyed by the flush rising up my neck.

"No problem." To my surprise, Sean was blushing, too.

The awkward moment was interrupted when the barking abruptly stopped. Inside, I heard the sound of shuffling feet growing closer. The lock rattled, but the door remained shut.

"Who's there?" a voice growled.

My throat went dry. I glanced from Connor to Sean, but they just looked back at me with wide eyes that seemed to say, *This was your idea, Cara.*

I swallowed hard. "It's Cara O'Reilly . . . Kathleen's granddaughter. And my sister Bri, and my cousin Connor and his friend Sean."

"Aye?" The door opened a crack. Jimmy glowered from the darkness of the cottage, his gaze roaming over each of our faces in turn. His scowl deepened. "I saw you three yesterday when that Lalor boy was attacking my tree. You friends with him?"

"No!" Connor and I exclaimed simultaneously.

"Ew, *Rob* Lalor?" Sean interrupted. "He's the worst. His dad's the one who wants to build that microplastics factory."

Jimmy opened the door a few inches more and eyed Sean appraisingly. "What do you know about that factory?" His teeth were yellow, and some were missing. One tooth protruded from his lips as he talked.

"I know it would be a disaster for the environment." Sean's voice rose as he pulled a flier from his backpack. "A microplastics factory would release all sorts of toxic chemicals into the air and water. Those chemicals could end up in everything we eat and drink. Plus, the working conditions can be really hazardous with a risk of chemical fires or spills." He thrust his flier at Jimmy, who took it with a bemused expression. "I'm organizing a school protest against the factory in a few weeks. Will you come?"

I stared at Sean, half-amused, half-impressed. Connor shot me a *told you so* look, and I grinned. Sean really was obsessed. But he knew his stuff, too.

Jimmy let out a little grunt of approval as he studied the flier. "Nice to see a kid who actually cares about our sacred land," he said somewhat grudgingly. Then he pulled the door open wider. "Come on in."

"Nice job," I whispered to Sean as we stepped inside, and he blushed.

A small white and brown Jack Russell terrier greeted us enthusiastically, jumping up to nip at my hand when I attempted to pet him. Jimmy ushered us into a dimly lit room, locking the door hastily behind us. He trudged over to the wood-burning stove, and I couldn't help noticing the way his trousers hung off his too-thin, almost shrunken frame. His worn jumper was so covered in rips and holes, it looked like a tug at one thread would cause the whole thing to unravel.

Stale smoke hung in the air, adding to the gloomy effect. Old black-and-white pictures hung crookedly on the walls, and the floor was covered in stacks of newspapers and farming magazines. The four of us stood awkwardly while Jimmy lowered himself slowly into an armchair next to the stove. The terrier leaped up into his lap, and Jimmy scratched it behind the ear while gesturing vaguely at a small sofa covered with a multicolored checked woolen blanket with his other hand.

"Go on, now, take a seat."

I looked at the sofa uncertainly. It was far too small for all four of us to squeeze in.

"Squawk." Bri held her raven straight out and navigated her way around the stacks of magazines. It almost looked like she was following the puppet. She reached the wall and grabbed a stool out from beneath a small table, dragged it to the other side of the stove, and sat.

"Hmm." Jimmy looked at my sister with a peculiar expression.

I glanced at Connor, who shrugged. Then he sat on one side of the couch. Sean sat on the other side, and I perched uncomfortably between them.

Jimmy's gaze moved over to me. His brow was slightly arched, but he said nothing.

I cleared my throat and tried to keep my voice from shaking. "Yesterday, you said something about a curse, and . . . and Ignis. What did you mean?"

Jimmy went very, very still. He stared at me unblinkingly for several long seconds. Then he leaned over, grabbed a log from the small pile next to the stove, and threw it on the fire. The flames shot up, casting light onto his cracked, wrinkled hands—and the freshly congealed blood on his right wrist.

Connor twitched next to me, and I knew he'd spotted it, too. I remembered Rob Lalor's huge, scary dog leaping for the branch, its powerful jaws clamping down on Jimmy's arm instead, and I shuddered. Why hadn't Jimmy cleaned and bandaged the wound?

Jimmy picked up a ceramic mug from the little table next to his armchair and took a long sip. He lowered the mug back onto the table, his hand shaking slightly. When he finally responded, his voice was a low croak barely audible over the crackling fire.

"Ignis and his shadow army will help the Formors destroy the Fae *and* the earthly realm. They'll plunge us all into darkness if we let 'em. Our minds cast shadows that we believe to be true . . . but the truth is the sparkle that lies beneath the shadow. Good thoughts channel the energy of the sparkle, but dark thoughts strengthen the deception, and cause despair. Best be careful with your thoughts."

Remember your thoughts have power, Cara. Pay attention to them.

My stomach roiled with nausea, and suddenly I regretted eating that scone. Dad had given me the very same warning right before he'd disappeared—before I'd wished him away. Maybe it was too late for me. Maybe I was already lost in darkness.

Jimmy continued, his gaze distant now. "This time of year, it's easier for the shadow army to pass into this realm and be seen by some. The veil is very thin, very thin indeed."

"The veil?" Sean said doubtfully.

Jimmy's eyes came into sharp focus now. "Some folk don't believe in the Fae, in the other realms. They're blind to the sparkle that connects us all. To live in the light, you need to free yourself from the shadow. When the veil is thin, it's easier to see the truth."

"I saw the Bow," I blurted out, and Jimmy's pale eyes fixed on me. "I . . . I have her comb. I wanted to return it last night, but it was high tide."

"Where did you find the comb?"

"I didn't," I said, glancing at Bri. "My sister did."

"Hmm." Jimmy gave Bri that same peculiar look, as if he were trying to analyze her. She stared back at him, her raven perfectly still in her lap. "There may be a reason for that."

"What do you mean?" I asked quickly.

Jimmy ignored my question. "You say you saw her. You saw into her realm. But to do that, you would need . . ."

He trailed off as I pulled out the fairy stone from beneath my shirt. "I found it in my gran's woodshed."

"No," Jimmy said with a small shake of his head. "You did not find it. It found you."

My heart skipped a beat.

Jimmy settled back into his armchair. "Return the comb, and the Bow may be able to help you fight Ignis."

I thought of Granny's warnings about Ignis in her journal. It sounded as though she'd met him before. "Is Ignis a person?"

Jimmy sighed, closing his eyes. "Ignis was once a person, but now he exists in the Otherworld as a dark energy. The only way to stop him is to bring more sparkle into this world, to help folks turn to the light. But getting that much sparkle requires no less than finding the door to the Otherworld and bringing the Stone of Destiny into this realm."

"I think that's what my dad was trying to do!" My voice was too high, but I couldn't help it. My heart raced out of control, and I could feel Connor and Sean both staring at me. "But Ignis . . . stopped him. Maybe even hurt him. And now there's a curse on our family."

Connor placed a gentle hand on my arm. I stared down at my trembling fingers, trying not to cry.

"Where's this door?" Connor asked.

Jimmy chuckled. "Well, there's a good question! I found one once when I was a wee boy. Took me to the most beautiful place, so full of sparkle. I met a Fae, I did—but I was acting the maggot and tried to catch the poor creature. See, I'd heard a story about fairies granting wishes. But this was a solitary Fae, not a trooping kind, and that type can be tricky. It threw me out of the Otherworld and put the stray on me so I didn't know where I was. The only way I found my way back home was by turning my coat inside out. Learned that trick from a tale my ma told me once!"

His laugh was more like a cackle. Next to me, Sean let out a nervous giggle.

"Well, the trick worked!" Jimmy finished. "I've searched for that door, many times since. But I can't remember for the life of me where it was."

I pulled my arm away from Connor's hand and forced myself to speak calmly. "I think my dad found a door on Carrauntoohil. He's been missing for almost a week now. He was trying to find the Stone of Destiny, but Ignis must have . . . stopped him."

Jimmy's smile faded. He let out a gusty sigh, scratching the top of his terrier's head. "I'm surprised he tried, if he knows the prophecy."

"Prophecy?" I repeated.

Jimmy's expression went cagey. He kept his eyes on his dog as he replied. "The Fae prophesied that the one who would bring the Stone of Destiny back to this realm would be a child."

I gaped at him. The word *Who?* began to form on my lips . . . and then I remembered Bri's drawing. The one I had thought was the mountain but was in fact the Stone of Destiny.

A chill ran through me despite the warmth of the fire. I looked at my sister, sitting there perfectly still on her stool with her raven puppet. Her familiar.

My sister, who stopped speaking before Dad's disappearance.

My sister, who drew the Bow.

My sister, who found her comb.

Dad said Bri had the gift of second sight. But what if her gift was even greater than that?

What if *Bri* was the child in the prophecy?

Fear slithered through me like a cold snake. If that were true, Ignis would come after her. Perhaps he already had, and *that* was the reason for her muteness. What else would he do to her? The thought of some dark Druid threatening my sister was too much to bear.

"Ignis is a trickster," Jimmy whispered, and my head snapped up. It was as if he'd read my mind. "Let him into your thoughts, and you'll be swallowed in darkness."

For a moment, the only sound in the room was the crackle of the fire. Then Jimmy gave the terrier a gentle shove, and it hopped off his lap. Heaving a sigh, Jimmy stood, his joints cracking loudly.

"There are many doors to the Otherworld, and you have a fairy stone to guide you," he said. "The Bow will also help if she deems you ripe for the quest . . . and you return her comb, of course. Now, it's best you be getting on with it, don't you think?"

He shuffled over to the door. Connor and Sean looked relieved as they stood to follow him. But I wasn't relieved. I was more worried than ever.

No one knew more about the Fae and the Formors than Dad and Granny. They must have known about the prophecy, too. Did they suspect Bri was the child? Was *that* why Dad had gone off to find the door and bring back the stone? The more I thought about it, the more it made sense. This must be the reason for all of the lies and secrets.

Bri was destined to bring back the Stone of Destiny and defeat Ignis. And that meant Ignis would stop at nothing to destroy her. Dad and Granny were just trying to protect us from the truth.

As we stepped outside into the harsh sunlight, Sean turned around.

"Jimmy, when you captured that Fae—what did you wish for?"

Jimmy cocked his head. "It was donkey's years ago. I was just a wee lad. I can't quite recall. I might've wished to go home, or asked for sweets . . ."

The terrier nipped at his ankle and let out an impatient *yap*.

Jimmy's face broke into a smile, displaying his full array of rotting teeth. "Or maybe I asked for a dog!"

He closed the door and bolted it shut. But as I followed the others through the yard of creepy gnomes, I could hear Jimmy's hoarse, cackling laugh behind us.

TEN

The Fairy Stone

WE RODE BACK to the base in silence. I breathed in the salty sea air, trying to shake the feeling of dread that had crept over me when Jimmy mentioned the prophecy. But even the sunshine and the cool fall breeze couldn't lift my spirits.

"I'm gonna grab some snacks," Connor said, hopping off his bike. "Meet you guys up in the base?"

"Sure," I said glumly. I didn't even want to think about eating.

"I'll go with you," Sean told Connor. They headed up the path together, talking in low enough voices that I couldn't hear them—which felt deliberate.

Yet another knot twisted itself up tight in my stomach. I had taken everything Jimmy Jo had said so seriously. But now that we were out of his creepy little cottage, with the sun shining overhead and the birds chirping merrily in the trees, I could see how it all must have sounded ridiculous. I felt my cheeks warm, remembering how my voice had cracked as I told Jimmy that Dad must have found a door to the Otherworld.

I'd hoped this visit would get Connor and Sean to understand it was all real. Instead, they probably thought I was just as weird as Jimmy Jo.

A tap on my shoulder caused me to jump. I whirled around and found myself face-to-face with Bri, her expression solemn.

"What?" I asked. It came out crankier than I'd intended, but I didn't apologize.

Bri reached into the inner pocket of her jacket and pulled out a neatly folded piece of paper. I shivered as I took it, but I didn't unfold it.

Another drawing. One she must have sketched before we left for Jimmy Jo's cottage. I was pretty sure I didn't want to see what it was.

"Can't you just *talk* to me instead of drawing all the time?" I asked desperately. "This is important, Bri. We have to work together. Can you say *anything*?"

"Squawk."

My fear bubbled over into frustration, and my hand shot out. I knocked the raven puppet off Bri's hand. It toppled to the ground at her feet.

Bri's eyes filled with tears, and instantly, I felt my own eyes grow hot, too.

"Bri, I'm sorry, I didn't mean to—"

But she swept up her raven and hurried into the house without giving me a chance to finish. I wiped my eyes quickly and turned to walk to the base.

Up in the tree house, I sat cross-legged against the wall and unfolded the drawing. The skin on the back of my neck prickled as the sight of the heavy black scribbles completely covering the page.

Darkness.

I heard footsteps and voices and hastily folded up the drawing and stuffed it into my pocket. A moment later, Connor climbed into the base with a bag of crisps clenched in his teeth. Sean followed with a box of cookies.

I avoided their eyes as they settled on the floor opposite me. Connor ripped the bag open and held it out to me. I shook my head, and he popped a handful of crisps into his mouth.

"Just say it," I said finally, unable to stand their silence anymore. Connor stopped chewing and stared at me. Sean froze with a cookie halfway to his mouth, his eyes darting between me and Connor as if he was watching a tennis match. "You think that was pointless. That Jimmy and I have both lost it."

Connor sighed, lowering the bag. "I don't think you've lost it," he said gently. "But I don't think all this stuff about curses and prophecies is *real*. I think you want to believe it's real because it's better than accepting that your dad is . . ." He trailed off, his cheeks reddening. "I mean, it's, um—"

"Go on," I said, a bitter taste rising in my throat like bile. "Better than accepting that Dad is *dead*."

"Cara—"

"You think he's dead," I said louder, and Sean flinched. "Fine. But I don't. I'm not giving up hope. And by the way, I don't hear you offering any other explanation about all the stuff that's going on. Dad disappearing, Bri going mute, the blackleg, Granny getting sick—if *all* of that isn't the curse, then what is it? A coincidence? Oh, and Bri's drawings, I guess those are a coincidence, too? She draws the Bow, then we meet her. She draws the Stone of Destiny, then—"

"She drew the Stone of Destiny?" Sean interrupted, leaning forward.

"Yes!" I said, sitting up straight. "I forgot to tell you guys about that. I thought she'd drawn Carrauntoohil, right? But last night, I found Granny's book on the Otherworld on my night table and in the back, there was a drawing of the Stone of Destiny. I was looking at Bri's drawing the wrong way. When I turned it sideways, it was almost a perfect match."

Connor frowned slightly. "You found the book in your room?"

"Yeah," I said. "Bri was asleep already. I think she put the book on my night table so that I'd see the picture and realize what *her* drawing actually was."

"Or . . ." Connor paused, looking almost apologetic. "Maybe Bri saw the picture of the stone and then drew her own. She could have found that book in Granny's study even before you did."

I squeezed my eyes closed and tried not to groan. "It's like you're looking for reasons not to believe in all of this!"

"Or maybe you're looking for reasons to believe in something that isn't real." Connor met my gaze evenly. "Cara, these are just stories Granny told us. Folklore. And . . . and I think maybe talking about all of this like it's real is scaring Bri."

"I'm looking after Bri," I retorted. "What if she's the child in the prophecy Jimmy Jo was talking about? The one who's supposed to defeat Ignis? That would explain why Dad was so desperate to get the Stone of Destiny first—he was trying to protect Bri. And that's why Granny and your mom keep brushing off all my questions about this stuff even though we *know* they actually believe in all of it!"

"We don't know that," Connor said with a sigh. "Just because you heard Granny say something about a curse doesn't mean she believes in *actual curses.* Or fairies, for that matter."

"And her journal? The photo with Frank and Miss F?"

"That's not proof of anything!" Connor sounded as though he was getting frustrated. "Granny's always been into Irish folklore. Your dad and my mom, too. But that *doesn't mean they actually believe it!*"

"Fine." I stood up abruptly. "Don't believe me. I'll take the comb back myself. I'll figure out how to save Dad. And I'll do it alone."

I stormed out of the tree house before either of them could see the tears welling in my eyes.

- ELEVEN -

The Shell

I FUMED ALL THE way back to the house. I couldn't help feeling betrayed. Even if Connor didn't believe in fairies and curses, shouldn't he at least offer to help me?

That's what he's trying to do, a little voice nagged in the back of my head. I ignored it.

"Cara!"

I looked up to see Aunt Jackie's car idling in the driveway. She poked her head out of the driver's window and smiled at me. Next to her, Bri sat in the passenger seat staring down at her lap.

"Aunt Jackie!" I said, jogging over to the car. "Is everything okay?"

"Just fine!" she replied with a smile. "Mom took a bath and had a little tea. She's taking a nap now—those antibiotics really take it out of her—so I thought I'd give her a little peace and quiet. Bri and I are taking a trip into Ballymore, if you want to join!"

I opened my mouth to say no then stopped. Did I really want to sit alone with my thoughts in a quiet house while Granny slept? Not really.

"Sure!"

I hopped into the backseat, and we were off. Aunt Jackie whistled cheerfully as she drove the winding road to Ballymore. I could see Bri's raven puppet in her lap, and I touched her lightly on the shoulder.

"Which shop do you think Corwin would like to visit?" I asked lightly. I still felt terrible for knocking the puppet off her hand earlier.

Bri ignored me, turning to stare out the window. We rode the rest of the way in silence.

Aunt Jackie found a parking spot across from a coffee shop. "I'm off to the market," she said as she climbed out of the car. "I noticed Mom's getting low on milk and a few other things. Meet me back here in half an hour or so?"

"Okay." I waved as Aunt Jackie headed down the street toward the market, then I turned to Bri. "So where do you want to . . ."

I trailed off because Bri wasn't there. Turning, I saw she was already heading down the street in the opposite direction of Aunt Jackie. I sighed heavily. Clearly, Bri wasn't ready to forgive me.

I headed in the direction of the harbor, where my favorite craft shop sat at the end of the lane. They sold a hodgepodge of artsy items made by locals, and I always found a unique souvenir or two.

Bells jangled when I pushed open the door, and I breathed in the familiar scent of potpourri and incense. The shop was empty, and I spent a few minutes browsing the little tables and shelves, examining bowls of colored stones, wind chimes made of driftwood, and watercolor paintings of different seascapes. I spotted a large white shell and picked it up, placing it against my right ear and listening to the gentle, almost distant sound of the ocean. When I lowered the shell, a voice right behind me caused me to jump.

"Do you hear the sea?"

I spun around, setting the shell down hastily. A lady I'd never seen before stood behind me, wearing a long green knitted cardigan and a small red knitted woolen cap. Long brown hair mingled with silver strands cascaded over her shoulders. She had a soft, pale face with green eyes that were unusually large.

"Um, y-yes," I stammered. I felt oddly guilty, even though I knew it was perfectly fine to touch things in this store.

"Was it musical?" she asked.

I blinked. "Uh . . ."

She smiled. "Try the other ear. You have to listen very, very carefully. The earth has music for those who know how to listen!"

Reluctantly, I held the shell over my left ear and listened to the same soft sea sound. I was about to lower the shell then stopped. Pressing the shell more firmly to my ear, I listened harder.

It was more than the distant roar of the ocean. The more I listened, the more I could hear tiers of sound—a high, soaring melody that faded in and out like waves lapping onto the shore, supported by a complex and ever-changing harmony layered like warm and cool currents—and beneath it all, a deep, steady bass. I focused on that low drone, and it grew louder and louder, the pitch sliding down ominously until it was so impossibly low, I felt it as a vibration in my chest.

I lowered the shell, gasping for breath as if I'd been underwater.

The lady was still there, watching me expectantly.

"I, I heard music," I managed to say. *And something else, too.*

She looked pleased. Her gaze moved to my neck, and she tilted her head. "Ah, I see you have a fairy stone to protect ye!"

My hand moved instinctively to the stone. "Yes. You . . . you know about fairy stones?"

Her laugh was like tinkling bells. "Aye, of course! Very lucky to find one—well, for one to find *you,* I should say.

The power of sight and protection from your fears, that's what a fairy stone gives ye. In the past, fishermen tied them to their boats. Some still do, but the old ways are dying, alas."

I rubbed the stone between my fingers. "My dad found this one, actually. I'm not sure exactly where."

"Mmm," she murmured. "Calms your mind to do that, doesn't it? May I?" She reached for the stone.

Reluctantly, I let go of it and nodded. I noticed with a start that her first two fingers were webbed together, but I tried not to react as she grazed the stone with her fingertips.

"That's a fine fairy stone you've got," she said at last, lowering her arm. "Keep it safe, now."

I smiled and promised I would, then hurried out of the shop. The lady had been nice enough, but that sound in the shell had left me feel unsettled and anxious. Remembering what Aunt Jackie taught me, I found a bench and sat, then closed my eyes and gripped the stone. *Breathe in peace and calm, one, two, three, four . . . breathe out worries and fear, one, two, three, four, five, six . . .*

I repeated the exercise a few times then opened my eyes. I felt strangely relaxed as I took in the harbor. A strong gust of wind blew in, rocking the boat masts and flapping the lines. Foamy waves crested again and again like white horses riding in from the sea.

My neck prickled, and I realized I could see someone in my peripheral vision, watching me. I glanced over at the corner and stiffened.

Rose.

She was alone this time, thankfully—I didn't much fancy another encounter with Rob Lalor and his horrible dog. But after the way Rose had told me off yesterday, I couldn't help feeling annoyed at the sight of her.

Standing, I shoved my hands in my pockets and began to walk in the other direction. But after a few steps, I heard her call, "Cara, wait!"

Heaving a sigh, I turned around.

Rose hurried across the street, coming to a stop in front of me. "Um . . . hi," she said, her cheeks tinged with pink.

"Hi," I said shortly. "What do you want?"

Rose bit her lip. "Look, I'm sorry about what I said yesterday. I have a lot going on right now, and I didn't know about . . . well, Rob told me about your dad after we left. I'm so sorry, Cara."

I glanced away, willing myself not to cry. "Thanks," I mumbled.

We stood there awkwardly for a moment, then Rose blurted out: "My parents are getting a divorce."

"Oh." I stared at her, unsure what to say. I wasn't completely surprised—Rose's dad had always been short-tempered and moody—but I didn't want to point that out.

Rose's blush deepened. "Not that that's anywhere near as awful as . . . as . . ." She ducked her head, flustered.

"As my dad being lost on a mountain?" I attempted a light-hearted tone and failed.

She glanced up, looking sheepish. "Well, yeah. In fact, I'm kind of relieved."

I let out a short laugh. She wanted her dad to leave, while all I wanted was for mine to come home.

"So, where's Rob today?" I said, changing the subject. I couldn't just stand here and talk about Dad, not without crying. And I was determined not to cry in front of Rose.

"I don't know," Rose replied uneasily.

"Looked like you guys were BFFs yesterday," I pointed out.

Rose made a face. "We're not. I mean, we're friends, but—I don't know what got into him, treating Jimmy Jo that way. I know I should've said something, or done something, but I . . . I felt helpless."

I looked at her pleading expression and felt my anger soften. "Yeah, I get it. I did, too."

Rose looked intensely relieved. "Rob can be okay some-times, but he's been acting weird lately. And my dad told me to stay on his good side. He's out of work right now and he's really hoping for a job at Mr. Lalor's factory." She caught my expression and frowned slightly. "What?"

"Nothing, just . . ." I pictured Sean handing Jimmy Jo the flier, his voice righteous with indignation as he talked about his protest. "A microplastics factory is gonna be kind of awful for the environment."

"Well, yeah," Rose admitted. "But my dad's desperate. Lots of people are. Things would be a lot better for me at home if my dad had work again."

I could see her point, and I wondered whether Sean knew how many people were relying on that factory for the same reason.

"Do you want to go trick or treating with me tomorrow?" Rose asked.

"Oh, um . . ." With everything that had been going on, I'd all but forgotten that tomorrow was Halloween. I still had to return the Bow's comb, not to mention figure out where the door to the Otherworld was to save my dad.

But the idea of doing something as normal as trick-or-treating with a friend was so appealing, I found myself saying, "Sure! That'd be fun."

"Cool," Rose said with a grin. "What's your costume?"

"Zombie tennis player," I told her. "I still gotta get some face paint and fake blood though."

"Me, too," Rose said. "Actually, Mom's driving me into town tomorrow morning to get everything I need. Wanna come?"

I hadn't actually thought about getting the rest of my supplies. Granny obviously couldn't take me, and I didn't want to ask Aunt Jackie when she had enough to worry about. "Yeah, that'd be fun!"

"Great!" Rose tucked a strand of hair behind her ear.

My gaze fell on the rainbow-colored cord tied around her wrist, and I smiled. "You've still got my friendship bracelet," I said, pointing. We'd swapped bracelets at the end of last summer. I still had her bracelet in my jewelry box.

"Oh, yeah." Rose lowered her arm, quickly tugging her jacket sleeve down over the bracelet. But not before I caught a glimpse of the deep bruises shaped like thumb prints on her wrist. "Well, I've to run. I'll call you later to let you know what time we'll be over in the morning to pick you up, okay?"

"Okay. See you later." I watched as Rose hurried off, trying not to picture those bruises or the expression on her face when she'd said things would be better for her at home if her dad had work.

Maybe Brian Lalor's factory getting built wouldn't be the worst thing after all.

- TWELVE -

The Monster

AUNT JACKIE DROPPED Bri and me off at home with a promise to be over in an hour to check on Granny and help prepare dinner. The house was deathly quiet, and after kicking off my shoes and hanging up my jacket, I went straight up to Granny's room.

I pushed the door open a crack and peered inside. Granny lay on her side, her back to me. Quietly, I crept into her room and made my way over to the bed.

"Granny?" I whispered.

She let out a soft, raspy exhale, and my shoulders slumped in relief. I pulled the blankets up over her shoulders then turned to go.

A soft shuffling noise caught my attention, and I froze. Then I saw Hugo the hedgehog in his crate, wiggling into a more comfortable position on his little bed. I walked over and knelt down next to the cage.

"Hugo," I said softly. "Hugo, you can hear me, right?"

The hedgehog didn't move.

"I know you talked to me before. You can talk. Can't you?"

He let out a loud snore that sounded fake. Either that, or I really was losing it.

"If you really are Granny's familiar, I need your help. Ignis has cursed all of us." I waited, watching the hedgehog closely.

At last, he rolled over and sat up with a world-weary sigh. Then he locked eyes with me and spoke. "Are you asking me to come on a quest?"

Even though I'd heard him speak before, this time was somehow even more shocking. Maybe because my argument with Connor really had me doubting everything I'd learned. My mouth opened and closed, but no sound came out.

"You look like a fish out of water, girl!" Hugo sounded cranky. "Is this a quest, yes or no?"

"Yes!" I finally managed to say.

"And how vital is this quest? How dangerous? How *epic*?"

"V-very!" I stammered. "It's a quest to, um, to find the door to the Otherworld."

"Hmm."

"And rescue my father."

"Hmm."

"And defeat Ignis and stop the Formors from spreading darkness in our realm!"

My voice rose higher than I'd intended, and I glanced over my shoulder at Granny. She still lay fast asleep. When I turned back, Hugo was curling back up on his bed.

"That's much too much for me," he informed me. "I'm old and stiff. Biggest quest I could manage would be a trip to the mailbox."

I gaped at him. "What?"

"You heard me!"

"You can't be serious!" I sputtered. "Granny is sick—aren't you her familiar? You're supposed to protect her!"

"I can't very well protect her if I'm sick, too!" The hedgehog lifted a tiny paw to his forehead. "Oh. *Ohhh.* Yes, I'm quite feverish. I must get my rest. Goodnight."

And with that, he rolled over and began to snore.

Unbelievable. I stood up and left Granny's room, closing the door softly behind me.

I found Bri in our room, sketching away in her art pad.

"Bri," I said. She didn't look up, and I sighed. "I said I'm sorry, and I meant it."

She half-shrugged and continued drawing.

"I looked at the picture you gave me," I said tentatively. "Could you explain what it's about?"

Another shrug.

"Was it about Dad? Or . . . or me?"

Nothing. I swallowed my frustration and sat on the end of her bed. Bri's pencil flew faster and faster, and I watched her with fascination. Finally, she dropped the pencil and turned her art pad around for me to see.

My blood ran cold.

It was her most intricate drawing yet—and the most terrifying. Most of the page was taken up by a great beast that seemed to be made entirely out of skulls. It loomed over a small figure, the black hole in the middle of its forehead glaring down. Leaning closer, I saw the figure was a young girl holding a baby, and my heart gave an extra-hard *thump*.

"Bri, is this . . . you?" I whispered hoarsely.

Bri let out a small sob and curled up on her side. The paper trembled in my hand, and I took a deep breath to steady myself. I stared at the girl clutching the tiny baby, and my heart flipped over. Was that my baby brother? But why would Bri have him when she faced Ignis? None of this made any sense.

But if this monster *was* Ignis . . . if this was what my sister was facing . . . I wouldn't let her face it alone.

Tomorrow was Halloween, the time of year when the veil would be at its thinnest. I was going to return the Bow's comb—and do whatever it took to convince her to help me save my family.

- THIRTEEN -

Miss F

I WOKE UP TO A TEXT from Rose. *Pick u up at 9:30?*
Smiling, I texted back a thumbs-up then yawned and sat
up. I'd checked the tides again last night before bed—
there was a low tide tonight. It would be my best chance to
return the comb to the Bow. The thought of going out to
Coffin Rock alone in the dark—much less actually asking the
Bow for help—sent chills up and down my arms. My dreams
had been filled with images of her bluish skin all creased like
a prune, the veins protruding from her bony hands, her eyes
like dark sunken holes with tiny pinpricks of light. Every time
I imagined approaching her, dread coiled in my stomach.

But I was determined to do whatever I had to do to keep
Bri safe and find my dad.

I dressed quietly, wondering whether Bri was still asleep or
just pretending. I hurried down the hall to check on Granny,
who was snoring peacefully. So was Hugo.

I glared at the hedgehog before closing the door. What would happen if I dragged Connor up here and tried to get Hugo to talk to him?

Probably nothing. Then Connor would *really* think something was wrong with me.

In the kitchen, I poured a bowl of cereal. I was trying so hard to pretend today was just a normal day of shopping with a friend and trick-or-treating for Halloween. But the reality of what I had to do tonight was sinking in, and with every minute that passed, I felt more and more jittery.

When Rose and her mom pulled up in her little red Honda, I did my best to sound upbeat and cheerful as I slid into the backseat. I chatted with Rose as we picked out face paint and fake blood at the toy shop. In the pharmacy, I pretended to be interested in helping Rose pick out a cat tail. And upstairs in the book shop, I dutifully followed Rose to the stationery section and listened as she explained how she was going to use cardboard to make a cat ear headband.

It was nice to hang out with Rose again. We had a lot of fun last summer. But today, I was having a hard time enjoying myself. It felt like a clock was ticking down the seconds until tonight, and with each *tick* that passed, my nerves grew more on edge.

When my phone buzzed in my pocket, I yelped so loud a few people turned to stare.

Rose stared at me, wide-eyed. "Are you okay?"

"Yeah, sorry," I said, feeling foolish. I pulled my phone out and saw a text from Connor.

Hey, I'm really sorry about yesterday.

I've just heard Miss F was moved from hospital to Skullageen nursing home. I'm heading there now with Sean to talk to her if you want to meet us there. We can ask her about the photo and the curse.

My throat tightened as I read it. I knew Connor still didn't believe me, but he was willing to listen. That was enough for now.

Thx. Meet you there.

"Cara, what's going on?"

I looked up to find Rose gazing at me with an odd expression. She seemed almost nervous.

"Nothing!" I said quickly. "That was just my cousin."

"It's just . . . if you don't want to hang out, I understand."

All morning I'd been on edge, and Rose thought it was because of her.

"No, I do!" I assured her hastily. "It's just—I have a lot going on right now. The whole thing with my dad is . . . complicated."

Rose nodded sympathetically. "I get that."

"Connor's going to visit this teacher who's in a nursing home," I said carefully. "And I want to meet him there. I need to talk to her. I know this is going to sound weird, but I think she might be able to help me figure out how to find my dad."

"Oh!" Rose said. "Sure, yeah. Let's go!"

I stared at her. "You want to come?"

"Of course!" she said. "This is obviously important to you."

For the first time that morning, I smiled for real. "Thanks, Rose. That's really nice of you."

She grinned. "Well, what are we waiting for? Let's go!"

⁓

Connor and Sean were sitting on the short wall outside the nursing home when Rose and I walked up the path.

"Hey, Cara," Connor said, giving me a sheepish smile. I noticed a box of chocolates on his lap. "Hi, Rose."

"Hi," I said. "Thanks for doing this."

"Yeah, of course!"

Connor hopped off the wall and headed to the entrance.

Sean trailed behind, walking next to me. "My cousin Sarah works here," he told me. "At the reception desk. Hopefully, that'll make it easier for us to visit with Miss F."

"Oh, cool." I noticed the tips of Sean's ears were pink for some reason. "Do they not allow visitors or something?"

"I think it's usually just family and close friends," he replied.

Behind the reception desk, a lanky teenage girl with thick fringe bangs glanced up from filing her nails. Her face brightened when she saw Sean. "Hey! What are you doing here?"

"Hi, Sarah!" Sean said, moving forward. "We wanted to visit Miss F. She was me and Connor's teacher, and we heard about the accident."

"We've got chocolates for her," Connor added, holding up the box.

"Oh yeah, Miss F—she's in room four." Sarah smacked her gum loudly. "But she's not allowed more visitors today. Orders from the manager."

"Just her?" I asked.

Sarah nodded. "This guy came to visit her this morning, and it didn't go well. She got really upset." Lowering her voice, she added, "Had to be sedated."

"Whoa." Sean's eyes were wide. "What'd he do to her?"

"No idea," Sarah replied. "Maybe nothing. Miss F's been having delusions, and she's super paranoid. Every time anyone goes in there to check on her, she thinks they're out to get her."

"Who was the visitor?" Connor asked.

Sarah shrugged. "Dunno. I wasn't on duty when it happened. Look, kiddo, the duty manager's gonna be back any second. I can't let you see her. Sorry."

"But—"

"It's fine," I said loudly, giving Sean a look. "We get it. Thanks anyway."

I led the way out of the nursing home. But instead of heading down the path to the sidewalk, I turned sharply and headed around the side of the building. Connor, Sean, and Rose hurried after me.

"Cara, what are you—"

"Here," I said, pointing to the door around the back. Through the window next to it, I could see the nursing home's small kitchen —it was empty. I pushed the door handle, and it turned easily.

"Uh . . ." said Sean.

"Hang on," Connor said, eyeing me. "If someone catches us, we could get in big trouble."

"I'll be the lookout," Rose said immediately. "Room four, right? If I see anyone, I'll come and warn you guys."

I felt a wave of gratitude toward my friend. "Thanks, Rose," I whispered. Then I slipped inside before Connor could say another word.

I walked down the hall, trying not to look guilty. "Remember, visitors are allowed to be here," I said over my shoulder to Connor and Sean. "No one will think we're up to anything unless we look like we are."

Connor nodded, his expression tense as we passed an elderly man edging down the corridor, hunched over a frame to steady himself.

"There it is," Sean whispered, pointing up ahead. I saw the number four on a glass panel next to a green door, glanced around to make sure the coast was clear, and reached for the door handle.

Sean reached for it at the same time, and his hand closed over mine.

We both pulled away quickly, mumbling apologies. As Sean entered the room first, I noticed his ears were bright red again. I followed him inside, the tips of my fingers vibrating. My vision went slightly blurry around the edges, and for a moment, I was terrified I was about to have another vision of that horrible darkness.

But this time was different. I felt a wave of emotion that wasn't my own wash over me like an ocean current. It was a warm, sort of giddy feeling, and it was coming from Sean.

Oh my god. I froze, staring at the back of his head. *Sean has a crush on me.*

I couldn't explain how I knew, even to myself. But I was absolutely certain that this feeling I was feeling was not mine but his. His feelings toward me.

Mortified, I turned my attention to Miss F. The bed was empty, and for a moment, I thought maybe this had all been for nothing and she wasn't even here. Then I spotted her in the rocking chair facing the window, gazing out at the bird feeders hanging from the trees outside. She had a crocheted blanket on her lap, and she rocked slowly back and forth.

"Miss F?" Sean moved forward, speaking softly. "Hi! It's Sean Ryan and Connor O'Brien from Skullageen Community School. Remember us?"

No reply. Sean looked helplessly from Connor to me.

"You know my mom, Jackie?" Connor tried. "She sent us with chocolates."

Still no response. But after a moment, I noticed Miss F's lips were moving. I walked closer, studying her. She looked so small and fragile, like an aged China doll. Her silver hair was pulled back into a neat ponytail. Her eyes were half-closed, but she was muttering something over and over again. I held my finger to my lips so Sean and Connor wouldn't say anything, and the three of us listened.

"Unicorn . . . goat and clover . . . turn to the left . . . through the stone."

I shivered as she repeated herself over and over again. Connor placed the box of chocolates on the table next to her chair as I pulled the photo from Granny's study from my backpack. Then I held it in front of Miss F.

"You and my gran were friends, too, Miss F," I said quietly. "I found this picture of you and her and Frank. And I need your help. My dad's missing, and I think you might know who's responsible."

Miss F stopped muttering and rocking. She stared unblinkingly at the photo through half-lidded eyes.

I swallowed hard. "I need you to tell me . . . who is Ignis?"

Tension hung in the air, thick as cobwebs. Miss F remained still as a statue for so long, I began to worry we might need to call a nurse.

Suddenly, her arm shot out. Her fingers closed tight around my wrist as she yanked my arm forward. Her eyes were wide open now, and when she spoke, it was in an urgent whisper.

"The one behind the lens is Ignis. He was here today to finish me off. Don't let the shadow obscure your light. Be strong." She squeezed harder, and I stifled a cry of pain. My heart was pounding so loudly in my ears that I barely heard what she said next. "You have her comb . . . give it back to her and she will help you."

She released me, and I stumbled back in shock, rubbing my wrist. Connor and Sean gaped at Miss F as she resumed her rocking, muttering the same words under her breath. *"Unicorn . . . goat and clover . . . turn to the left . . . through the stone."*

I realized I was trembling from head to toe. When the door opened, I nearly jumped out of my skin.

Rose stuck her head into the room. "The manager's back!" she hissed, clearly panicked.

With a last look at Miss F, I followed Connor and Sean out into the hall.

"We have to see who that visitor was," I said. I half-expected Connor to argue, but he nodded in agreement.

"I'll do it," Sean said. "There's got to be a visitor log or something. I'll meet you guys outside."

"Thanks, Sean," I said fervently, and this time he blushed right to the roots of his hair.

Connor, Rose, and I hurried to the kitchen and out the back door. When we rounded the corner of the nursing home, Sean was already walking out of the front doors. He had an odd expression on his face, but he didn't say anything until we all reached the sidewalk.

"Well?" I asked eagerly. "Did you find out who visited Miss F?"

He nodded. "It was Mr. Lalor."

My mouth fell open, and I couldn't help glancing at Rose. She looked equally startled. "Rob's dad?" she asked.

"Yeah. Brian Lalor. The guy who wants to build a microplastics factory." Sean made a face. "Apparently that's not evil enough, so he's threatening sweet old teachers with head injuries, too."

Rose looked down at her feet, clearly uncomfortable. I realized Sean didn't know about her strange friendship with Rob or the fact that her dad was relying on that factory getting built so he could have a job.

I cleared my throat. "So, Miss F thinks Brian Lalor is Ignis."

"To be fair, Sarah said Miss F has been acting paranoid about pretty much everyone," Connor pointed out. "Plus, didn't Miss F say the person who took that photo was Ignis?"

"Yeah, so?"

"So, think about how young Granny is in it! That was like, thirty-something years ago. Brian Lalor would've been a child."

"Oh, right." I chewed my lip, trying to think. Maybe Miss F really was just delusional and this didn't mean anything, but when I thought about the look in her eyes and the intensity of her voice as she'd told me about Ignis, I didn't think she looked delusional at all.

She'd looked terrified.

"What photo?" Rose asked in a funny voice.

Wordlessly, I pulled out the picture of Granny, Miss F, and Frank.

She bit her lip. "You said this was taken about thirty years ago?"

"Something like that, yeah. Why?"

"Because . . ." Rose took a deep breath. "Because that's right around when Rob's granddad disappeared."

A zip of electricity raced through me. "He *disappeared*?"

"Yeah. Rob told me. That's all I know," she added hastily. "That and his granddad's name was Dubhan."

"Miss F's pretty out of it," Sean said. "If Brian Lalor looks like his dad did thirty years ago, she might've thought he was Dubhan this morning. Maybe that's why she got so scared!"

I exhaled slowly, looking down at the photo. Granny and Miss F smiled happily while Frank glowered. I pictured a fourth person, an older version of Rob, holding the camera and snapping the shot. *Druids are magicians who work with sparkle, and most help those who are full of darkness. But there is one whom the Fae fear.*

"Guys," I whispered. "I think Dubhan Lalor is Ignis."

- FOURTEEN -

The Comb

AUNT JACKIE PICKED us up in front of the pharmacy down the street from the nursing home. She made chit chat with Rose and Sean while Connor stayed mostly silent, occasionally trying to catch my eye. I avoided his gaze, turning my attention to the trees whizzing past outside the window. I was still trying to absorb what I'd just learned.

Rob Lalor's granddad was Ignis.

Back at the base, the four of us sat in a circle on the floor. Wind howled through the tree house windows, and I could hear the trees groan and creak outside.

"So," Rose said at last. "Want to fill me in on what this is all about?"

I hesitated, glancing at Connor. I could tell he didn't completely trust her either, not after the incident with Rob and Jimmy Jo. But I reminded myself that Rose was in a tough situation at home, and she really did seem to regret what she'd said.

"You have to promise not to tell anyone," I told her, and she nodded vigorously.

"Especially not Rob," Connor added.

Rose's cheeks reddened. "I won't."

I drew a deep breath then told her everything: the Stone of Destiny, my dad's note, the Bow and her comb, Granny's notes on the Druids, the old story about Ignis and the Formors.

"And you think Ignis is Rob's granddad?" Rose asked.

I nodded. "He's the right age. Plus, why else would Brian Lalor randomly threaten Miss F? He's helping his dad. She's under Ignis's curse, just like my dad and gran."

"And Frank, too, maybe," Sean added, looking at me intently. "He was in the photo. Plus, you said he was yelling about a curse to your gran the other day."

"Exactly," I said, not quite meeting his eyes. Sean sounded like he was totally on board with all of this now. But did he really believe me, or was he just pretending to because he . . . *liked* me?

Connor leaned against the wall, turning his cap backward. "Okay, let's think about this rationally. Granny, Frank, Miss F, and a fourth person who could have been Dubhan Lalor used to meet together to . . ." He paused, wrinkling his nose.

"Well, do what, exactly? We don't know, but it has something to do with Druids, according to that photo."

I looked at the picture again. This time, instead of studying the people, I looked at their surroundings. "There's a church steeple in the distance behind them," I said slowly. "And it looks like they're next to a wooded area."

"What was it Miss F kept saying over and over again?" Sean asked. "Something about a unicorn?"

"Unicorn, goat and clover, turn to the left, through the door," I replied immediately. I could still hear Miss F's raspy voice whispering those words over and over.

"There's a pub on the way to Skullageen called Goat and Clover," Sean said excitedly. "It's just before the church!"

"Oh yeah!" Rose sat up straighter. "And before the pub, there's a unicorn road sign!"

My heart began to race. "What about *on the left*? What's on the left after the pub?"

Sean frowned as he thought. Then his eyes widened dramatically. "The site of Brian Lalor's microplastics factory."

We sat in stunned silence for a moment.

"Unicorn, goat and clover, turn to the left . . . *through the door*." I stared at each of them in turn. "Guys, the door to the Otherworld is somewhere on the site. *That's* why Brian Lalor wants to build there! He's helping Ignis conceal the door forever so no one can find the Stone of Destiny!"

"Whoa." Sean let out a slow breath. "Okay. So now what do we do?"

"What Granny and Miss F told me to do," I said firmly. "I have to return the Bow's comb. I need her help."

"Cara . . ." Connor started, then paused.

I crossed my arms and glared at him. "What? Still don't believe in this stuff?"

"Well . . . I mean, obviously something weird is going on. But that doesn't mean the Fae are real."

"Yeah, I might think that, too, if I hadn't seen the Bow myself." I pulled out the fairy stone around my neck and squeezed it. "I saw her, Connor. I *know* the Fae are real. And I heard the three knocks."

"Three knocks?" Rose asked.

I pounded the wooden floor with my fist three times. *Thud. Thud. Thud.*

"I heard that on our front door and opened it," I told them. "No one was there. When the Bow knocks three times, it means someone will *die.* So, I'm not going to waste any more time trying to convince you guys she's real. It's low tide tonight, and I'm going to Coffin Rock to return the comb."

"Tonight?" Connor repeated. "But—"

"Tonight is when the veil between worlds is thinnest," I said stubbornly. "It has to be tonight."

"Yeah, but Cara, there's a massive storm forecast tonight," Connor said. "Low tide or not, it's gonna be impossible to get to Coffin Rock."

My heart sank, but I kept my chin up. "Not impossible, just difficult. Don't you get it, Connor? I don't have a choice!"

For a moment, he looked as if he wanted to argue. Then he shook his head. "Then I'm coming with you."

"Me, too," Sean added quickly.

Rose nodded. "Same here. No way are you doing this alone, Cara."

I was touched—and a little horrified to realize my eyes were filling with tears. "Thanks, guys," I said, ducking my head and pretending to check the time on my phone. "We should do this now before the storm gets here."

"But when I texted my mom to tell her I was coming here, she said she'd pick me up at three," Rose said. "I have to get my costume ready. Not that that's more important than this," she added hastily. "But I don't know what she'd say if I texted her that I was going out to Coffin Rock to give a comb to a fairy."

"Same here," Connor admitted. "I don't think Mom would let me do this."

"Okay, new plan," I said. "We'll get our costumes on like this is a normal Halloween so the adults don't catch on. Meet back here in an hour?"

"Sounds good," Connor said.

"Let's do this!" Sean actually sounded excited. He put his fist out in front of me, and Connor put his fist on top. Laughing, I put my fist on top of Connor's. After a moment, Rose put her hand on top, giving me a sheepish smile.

"We're like the Avengers!" Sean said with a grin. "Only instead of Thanos, we're gonna take Ignis down."

Connor and Rose cracked up, but in that moment, I really believed Sean. We were going to do this.

And I was going to save my dad.

⌒ᔓ

Forty-five minutes later, I checked my reflection in the bathroom mirror. I'd cut holes in my white tennis top and skirt then spattered them with the fake blood I'd bought at the pharmacy. My face was covered in white paint, with more blood dripping from my mouth and the corners of my eyes. My hair was in pigtails with a few streaks of fake blood, and I wore my sweatband over my head, although it looked more like a bandage covering a bloody wound.

"Squawk!"

I gasped and whirled around. Bri stood in the doorway wearing her skeleton outfit, Corwin the raven perched on her hand.

"Bri!" I said, putting a hand to my chest. "You scared me."

She gazed at me, her eyes huge saucers. Her mouth was turned down at the corners. My eyes fell on the paper in her free hand, and I stifled a groan.

"Is that for me?"

She nodded, handing me the picture. I unfolded it, my shoulders slumping with relief when I saw it was a sketch of the fairy stone.

"Don't worry!" I told her, touching the cord around my neck. "I've got it."

Bri looked down at her feet. After a moment, I moved past her and headed to our room. I grabbed my tennis racket then opened my sock drawer and pulled out the comb. My heart thumped extra hard as I stared at it, remembering the way the Bow had reached for it with her claw-like hand. I tucked it carefully into the inner pocket of my rucksack then stuffed the tennis racket inside and zipped it up.

I checked on Granny, who was actually sitting up in bed reading a book. Her face was still too pale, but otherwise she looked better.

"What an excellent costume," she said, smiling weakly at me. "Have fun tonight, Cara."

"I will," I said, trying to sound bright and cheerful.

Downstairs, I put on my jacket and boots. I was about to open the front door when something in the kitchen caught my attention.

I turned slowly. I couldn't quite pinpoint what it was—a sight? a sound?—but something compelled me to go into the kitchen and investigate. I stood near the table, looking around at the oven, the refrigerator, the cupboards, the shelf with Granny's baking things . . . *there.*

My eyes locked onto a clean empty jam jar. I could sense a sort of energy emanating from it. It was as if the jar were trying to communicate with me . . . which was ridiculous. I was about to leave when I heard Dad's voice.

Remember your thoughts have power, Cara. Pay attention to them.

Straightening my shoulders, I marched over to the shelf, grabbed the jam jar, and stuffed it into my rucksack. Then I headed out the door.

I was halfway down the path when the front door banged behind me. Bri came hurrying down the porch steps after me, and I grimaced.

"No, Bri, I'm not actually going trick-or-treating," I said in the gentlest voice I could manage. "I'm bringing the Bow's comb back. You can't come."

She stared at me with that stubborn frown I knew so well.

"It's too dangerous," I said firmly. "You have to stay home."

"Squawk."

"Bri, you can't—"

"Squawk!" Bri's voice cracked, and her eyes filled with tears.

Instantly, I felt guilty. "Fine." I sighed. "But you aren't going anywhere near the Bow. Got it?"

She nodded, and we headed to the base together.

Connor and Sean were already there, and their Batman and Robin costumes made me smile despite what we were about to do.

"Time to save the day, right?" I joked weakly, and Connor laughed.

"Hey, we've got a Catwoman!" Sean said excitedly, pointing. I turned as Rose strolled up in her black leotard, complete with black painted nose, whiskers, tail, and pointy-ear headband.

"You, look great," I told her.

She smiled. "You too."

"Do you have the comb?" Connor asked me.

In response, I pulled the comb out of my rucksack pocket and held it out. It glistened in my hand like a luminescent pearl.

The others gazed in wonder.

"It's beautiful," Rose whispered. "No wonder she wants it back."

The distant, low rumble of thunder sent my hand grasping for the fairy stone as I noticed goose bumps erupt on my skin. I looked up at the sky—still clear overhead, but I could see dark clouds gathering on the horizon.

"Well, let's get this over with," I said. "Connor, I'm going to need a kayak just in case the water's still high."

"No problem." We walked over to Uncle Pat's small wooden kayak shed. Inside, Connor lifted one kayak from a shelf and handed it to me. Then he pulled down a second kayak.

"I only need one," I said, confused.

He rolled his eyes. "Cara, I said I'm with you, didn't I?"

"Yeah, but you don't have to actually come out to—"

"Well, I'm going to. No arguments." He grabbed two life vests off a shelf and handed me one.

"Thanks," I said as I slipped it on. "For doing this, I mean."

"Anytime." Connor grinned at me. His Batman costume looked extra ridiculous with the ancient orange life vest buckled over it. "Besides, if the Bow *is* real, I'm gonna need to see her for myself." He dragged his kayak out of the shed.

Smiling, I followed him.

We headed to Dead Man's Cove, Connor and I dragging our kayaks behind us. Connor, Sean, and Rose kept up a steady stream of conversation, but I didn't join in. It was only a quarter after four o'clock, but already the sky was darkening. And I didn't like the looks of the storm clouds in the distance—they seemed to be rolling in unnaturally fast.

The chatter stopped when we reached the cove. I pulled my kayak to the shore then took the comb out of my rucksack and tucked it carefully into my jacket pocket underneath the life vest.

Thunder boomed, causing Rose to let out a nervous squeak. "Are you sure this is safe?" she asked, looking from Connor to me.

"No," I admitted. "But the longer we wait, the less safe it'll be."

I started to push my kayak out onto the water but stopped when Bri gripped my arm.

"Squawk!"

She stared pleadingly into my eyes, her fingers squeezing so hard I almost cried out.

"Bri, it's gonna be alright," I said in the most reassuring voice I could manage.

Her lips wobbled, and for a moment, I thought she would burst into tears. But then she let go of me and stepped back.

I climbed into my kayak, and Connor climbed into his. Rose and Sean stood behind us, and I took a deep breath. "Go!"

Rose gave my kayak a shove. Next to us, Sean did the same for Connor. We drifted out onto the water, and I picked up the paddle and tried to keep my hands from shaking.

Coffin Rock sat around the headland. As Connor and I paddled, a few seals popped up to investigate our kayaks, snorting heavily and splashing us with their tails. Once we made it around the headland, the current became much stronger. I struggled to use the paddle in the suddenly choppy waves.

Glancing over, I noticed Connor's kayak drifting further away from me.

The storm clouds had almost reached us, and a fat, cold rain drop hit my forehead. The soft pink late afternoon light was swallowed in swirls of gray. A fog rolled in over the water, and I swore I could physically feel its heaviness settled over me like a blanket.

This was no ordinary storm.

"Connor!" I yelled, my kayak rocking back and forth. "Can you see the rock?"

No response. I dropped the paddle next to my feet and grabbed the edges of my kayak as another wave rocked it even more violently. I couldn't see Coffin Rock, I couldn't see Connor . . . the dark, supernatural fog had closed in on me.

"Connor!" I screamed. I never should have let him come. He didn't have his glasses, and he'd never be able to find his way back to shore. A wave crested over my kayak, slapping me right in the face. I coughed and sputtered the cold, salty water and looked around frantically.

"Cara . . . Cara . . . Cara . . ."

I felt numb from head to toe. That wasn't Connor's voice.

I began to see faces in the fog, warped and twisted with long oval mouths in permanent screams. Something dark brushed past me, and I could sense its menace.

Ignis.

Underneath the sound of the waves and the rain now beating down, a distant wailing reached my ears. *The Bow.* I grabbed up the paddle and began steering the kayak in the direction of the wails, but it was hopeless. The waves would take me where they pleased. My arm muscles screamed with effort as I slammed the paddle into the water over and over. Through the fog, I saw something looming high overhead. For a blissful moment, I thought it was Coffin Rock.

Then I realized it was a massive wave. I sucked in a deep breath a split second before it crashed down on me.

The force of the wave shoved me deep in the cold water. I nearly screamed when something slick and slimy closed around me—seaweed. My life vest came loose, and I reached for the pocket that held the comb. I would not let Ignis take it from me.

No sooner did I think that then I felt the cord around my neck snap. My hand flew up, but it was too late—the fairy stone hovered in front of my eyes for a brief moment before a current swept it away.

It's over.

I can't stop bad things from happening.

I cause them to happen.

I'm cursed.

I am darkness.

I squeezed my eyes tight shut as more awful thoughts clouded my mind. My lungs felt as though they might burst any moment. And so what if they did? This was all my fault. Connor had likely capsized. Dad was gone. All Ignis had to do was drown me, and no one would be able to stop him from going after Bri. Then the Stone of Destiny would be his, and darkness would take over the world. It was over. I was powerless.

I drifted down, down, down into the murky depths. But it wasn't only water that was enveloping me in its cold embrace. It was my own dark thoughts.

Ignis is a trickster . . . Let him into your thoughts, and you'll be swallowed in darkness.

I opened my eyes.

The saltwater stung, but I blinked and looked up. The surface wasn't as far away as I'd feared, but I couldn't fight the current. I pumped my arms hard, spinning to face the other direction—and found myself face to face with the lady from the craft shop.

I've lost it, I thought. She wore her little red cap, long hair swirling around her face, those huge eyes sparkling with emerald light. Only now dark green scales covered her arms and neck, and when I looked down, I realized she had a fish tail instead of legs.

Sea fairy. I struggled to recall Dad's story. *Merrow.*

The merrow smiled at me, holding out her webbed hand. And there in her palm was my fairy stone. *"Shine bright,"* she said clearly, her eyes sparkling.

I grasped the stone tightly, and warmth surrounded me. At that moment, though I knew it was impossible, I felt Dad wrap his arms around me and hug me tightly. A surge of energy flowed through me, bright and hopeful, and a new thought sprang into my mind, driving out all of the darkness.

I am a warrior of light!

Brightness surrounded me, and I found myself speeding toward the surface, leaving the merrow behind. I sucked in cold air and coughed hoarsely. Over the storm now raging, I could hear the Bow's wailing—and she was close.

"Cara!"

I gasped, choking on a mouthful of saltwater. "Connor?"

"Here!"

I turned and spotted him in his kayak not far from me, and I went weak with relief. I swam over as fast as I could and grabbed his hand.

"You're okay!" I said, half-laughing, half-crying.

"I saw your kayak capsize," he said, squeezing it back. "I tried to get to you when you fell out . . . I was so worried!"

Connor held his kayak as steady as possible so I could climb on. I grabbed his arms and he heaved me inside. For a moment, I perched there, panting and sopping wet, shivering but alive. Then I grabbed my paddle that floated nearby.

"We're close to the rock," I said grimly. "Let's give the Bow what she wants and end this."

- FIFTEEN -

Shine Bright

CONNOR AND I PADDLED the kayak together. My arm muscles burned from the effort of fighting the current and balancing. But I could hear the Bow's wails getting closer, and I gritted my teeth and kept paddling.

"Whoa, what in the world?!" Connor shouted behind me.

I turned, half-expecting to see the Bow herself. But instead, I spotted a familiar face out in the water near our kayak. She smiled and waved a webbed hand before diving back into the deep.

"That's a merrow," I called to Connor over the sound of the storm. "Don't worry, she's light, not darkness. She also works at the craft shop."

Connor gaped at me. *"What?"*

I almost laughed. "Never mind, let's just get to Coffin Rock!"

"But we can't see a thing!" Connor said, wiping droplets from his Batman mask.

"That's it!" I released the paddle and grabbed the fairy stone. My fingers fumbled as I tied a new knot in the cord, then slipped it over my head before lifting the stone to my eye.

The mist dissipated, replaced with a bright shimmer that covered the waves. I spotted a dark shape in all the light, and as it came more into focus, I recognized the shape of Coffin Rock. The Bow stood on top, and as if she knew I was watching, she turned to face me. Her piercing eyes shone as they locked onto mine, and I dropped the stone to my chest.. Instantly, the world went dark and misty again.

"That way," I gasped, pointing.

Connor said nothing but helped me paddle in the direction of the rock. It felt like trying to paddle through mud, but we worked together, finding a rhythm, and the Bow's wails grew to an unbearable pitch until finally—

"Oof," Connor grunted as the kayak bumped into the rock.

"Keep us steady!" I yelled, and Connor reached out and grabbed a jagged section of the rock so we wouldn't drift away. The kayak continued thumping against the side as I dug the comb out of my pocket. I was about to lift the fairy stone to my eye again when the wailing abruptly stopped. Then Connor let out a shrill shriek.

I looked up and felt all the breath whoosh from my lungs.

The Bow leaned over the top of the rock, her hooded face an arm's length away. The pinpricks of light in her black eyes glinted hungrily.

"H-here's your comb," I said shakily, holding it up.

That claw-like hand lunged forward, snatching up the comb.

I reeled back, nearly losing my balance as the Bow retreated back into the mist on top of the rock.

"Let's get out of here!" Connor's voice was unusually high as he fumbled with his oar.

But I wasn't ready. "Wait, please!" I called desperately after the Bow. "I need your help. I have to find the door to the Otherworld to stop Ignis and save my dad. Please, will you help me?"

Squinting, I could still make out the Bow's silhouette on top of the rock. Her hooded head dipped once. A nod. *Yes.*

Then she disappeared.

Almost immediately, the mist began to recede, and the water grew calm. A sense of peace descended over me as I sat back down on the kayak.

Connor pushed off the rock with his paddle, and we rowed our way back to shore in silence. By the time we reached the pebble beach, the darkness of the storm had dispersed, and the calm water reflected a blood orange sky.

Rose and Sean hurried toward us, their expressions relieved.

"That storm came out of nowhere!" Sean yelled. "All of a sudden, we couldn't see you guys anymore!"

"We had to wait it out under there," Rose added, helping me out of the kayak. I looked and saw a rickety old shack down the beach. "We were so scared for you guys! Are you okay?"

"Yeah, I think so," I said, glancing down at myself. "Although I guess I'm just a regular tennis player now. All the fake blood must've washed away when I fell out of my kayak."

"You fell out?" Sean and Rose cried in unison.

I started to giggle, and they looked at me in alarm. But I couldn't help it. I felt giddy with relief. "I did, but a merrow saved me. Then we found Coffin Rock and gave the Bow back her comb."

"A *merrow*?" Rose asked.

"You saw the Bow?" Sean exclaimed.

"If you don't believe me, ask Connor!" I said, grinning at him.

My cousin hadn't said a word since we'd reached shore. He stood there, blinking water out of his eyes, his Batman mask askew and a strand of seaweed dangling from his utility belt.

"Yeah," he said at last, his voice weak. "I saw her. The Bow is real. It's all . . . *real*."

Sean let out a whoop that caused a seagull perched on a piece of driftwood nearby to take flight in alarm.

I started laughing again—I couldn't help it. I knew I still had Ignis to worry about. I still had to figure out how to save my dad.

But I'd returned the comb. The Bow was on my side. And maybe best of all, Connor *finally* believed me.

Rose looked stunned. "Wow," she whispered. "Oh, *wow.*"

"What does the Bow look like?" Sean asked eagerly.

"Exactly like Bri's drawing," I said. "She's got . . . wait, where's Bri?"

Silence fell as the four of us looked around.

"She ran back to the shack with us when it started to rain," Rose said uneasily. "The three of us stood just inside there . . ."

I was already running to the shack. But when I reached it, I immediately saw it was empty.

"We came running out when we saw you coming," Sean told me, his brow furrowed. "I thought Bri was with us, but . . ."

My intense relief had faded, replaced with a rapidly growing dread. I could feel the darkness closing in on me again, just as it had out on the water.

Then I remembered that bright, beautiful energy that had filled me the moment I felt Dad wrap his arms around me.

"Shine bright," I whispered.

Connor frowned at me. "Huh?"

"Jimmy Jo told us that Ignis tricks you by getting into your thoughts," I said, speaking more to myself than to him. "He's a trickster. The only way to beat him is to shine bright—to not let shadows take over my thoughts. I have to keep my thoughts positive if I'm going to dwell in the light."

"You have to be a flame!" Sean said.

I looked at him, startled. "What do you mean?"

"Flames don't cast a shadow because they're a source of light," he explained. "If you're the source of light, you know any darkness or negative thoughts are just an illusion, and you don't allow them to get in the way of your light."

I felt a smile spread across my face. "Yeah. Like that."

Sean grinned back at me, a blush creeping up his neck.

"Let's go to Granny's and get cleaned up," I said as my body shook. "Bri's probably there. And if not . . ." I paused, trying to ignore the knot of worry in my stomach. "If not, we'll find her."

We walked back to the farmhouse. Connor seemed to be recovering from the shock, and he and Sean launched into an animated discussion about the Fae and what other supernatural creatures may or may not be real.

Rose, on the other hand, was strangely silent. Her face was pale beneath the paint, and I could see her texting on her phone—probably checking in with her mom. When I put my hand on her shoulder, she jumped in fright.

"Sorry," I said, dropping my hand. "Are you okay?"

"Yes! Fine." She let out a funny-sounding laugh. "This is all just a lot to take in. I mean . . . fairies."

"Yeah." I tried to smile, but my thoughts were still on Bri.

When we reached the gate, I broke into a run. "Bri? Bri!" I called as soon as I entered. I checked the living room and the kitchen before hurrying upstairs. My stomach sank when I saw our bedroom was empty. I peeked in Granny's room and found her asleep. The study was empty as well. I returned to my room, intending to change out of my sopping wet costume—and that was when I spotted the drawing on my bed.

I snatched it up and stared at the picture, my heart hammering. Then I turned around and rushed back downstairs.

Connor, Sean, and Rose looked up in alarm as I waved the paper at them.

"We need to go see Frank."

- SIXTEEN -

The Pooka

FIFTEEN MINUTES LATER, Connor's older brother Eoin pulled up in his tiny green Volkswagen. A song I vaguely recognized was cranked up on the radio, and the whole car seemed to vibrate along with the bass.

Connor sat in the front passenger seat. After calling Eoin to ask for a ride, he'd rummaged around in Granny's closets until he found a pair of his old sweatpants and sweatshirt that still fit him. I had changed into dry clothes, too, after he practically ordered me.

"We're not going to find Bri any faster if we freeze to death in these wet clothes, Cara," Connor had said in a tone that reminded me forcibly of Aunt Jackie. "You should really eat something, too."

Now, Connor and Sean chomped down on hastily made turkey and cheese sandwiches. The way my stomach was roiling with nerves, I couldn't even think about eating. I clutched Granny's photo in my hands, along with the drawing of the old man. Bri had sketched him with his back to her, his face obscured, but I knew it must be Frank. He was always at that pub in Ballymore.

Apparently, Rose had no interest in tracking down Frank. After I returned from changing my clothes, Sean informed me that Rose had bailed.

"She can't walk home from here—it's too far!" I exclaimed.

Sean shook his head. "There was a car coming up the road—she said it was her mom. Must've texted her without telling us."

I remembered the way Rose had furtively typed on her phone as we'd walked back from the shore. She must have been really scared, I realized, feeling a small wave of guilt for dragging her into this.

At last, Eoin's car pulled up to the pub, a squat building made of gray stone with a colored glass door and a sign reading FOLEY'S.

"Thanks, Eoin!" I called as we hopped out and slammed the doors.

"We'll only be a few minutes," Connor added.

Eoin flashed a smile then rolled up his window and cranked up the radio even louder.

Inside, I scanned the place for Bri. The pub was dimly lit, with a faded red interior, but it took only two seconds for me to see she wasn't there. My stomach sank.

"There's Frank," Connor said grimly. I spotted him too—a lone figure at the bar, a half-full pint of Guinness in his hand. I felt the same shiver of fear as I did every time I saw him, but I couldn't afford to let my fear get the better of me now. Not with Bri missing.

As I marched over to the bar, Frank turned slowly. As always, his wiry hair was pulled into a loose ponytail, and a black patch covered his left eye. His right eye locked onto me, and he smirked.

"What would Kathleen say if she saw you here?"

I ignored the jibe and held out the photo. "Who took this picture? Was it Ignis?"

Frank stared at the image, the smile vanishing from his face. He took a big gulp of Guinness, then another, until he'd drained the pint. Then he set the glass down with a heavy *thud* on the bar and swiveled around in his stool to face me.

"His name wasn't always Ignis," he said slowly. "The four of us formed the Ballymore Grove of Druids years ago. We wanted to work with the Fae to bring more sparkle into the world. Each of us specialized in one of the four elements: your granny's was earth, Mary's was air, I worked with water, and . . . *he* worked with fire."

I swallowed hard. Next to me, Connor and Sean listened with wide eyes.

"We started calling him Ignis as a joke of sorts." Frank let out a raspy chuckle. "Always playing with fire, that one. Igniting the darkness. His skill could have helped the world, but it could also cause great suffering . . . and unfortunately, the power of that sort of dark magic, Formors magic, it proved too much of a temptation. We grew worried. And then . . . we grew afraid."

Frank took the photo from my hands. He seemed lost in his memories now, barely aware of us standing there.

"He wanted to join the Formors. Grow his power. Swore he'd use it for good, but we knew better. We asked him to leave the group, to put a stop to his meddling with the Formors, and he became . . . angry. Cursed each one of us then disappeared into the Otherworld."

"He cursed you?" I whispered.

Frank looked up. His eye was bloodshot.

"I had a fishing accident. Lost this." He gestured to his eye patch, and I shuddered. "Mary lost a child. Your granny . . . well, she lost your granddad, didn't she?"

My mouth fell open. "That was a farming accident!" I said automatically.

Frank drummed his fingers on the bar. "'Twas no accident, girl. You can thank Ignis for that."

I took a deep breath. "You mean Dubhan Lalor?"

Frank's fingers stopped drumming. He was silent for so long, I started to think he hadn't heard me. Then he whispered, "Yes. Dubhan."

Even though I wasn't surprised, a chill ran through me.

"Now his son's building a factory on the site of the door to the Otherworld," I said, the words spilling out in a rush. "That way, no one can find the Stone of Destiny. Not even my sister."

Frank squinted at me. "Your sister?"

"Yes, Bri." Just saying her name sent a fresh wave of fear through me. "I think she's the child in the prophecy. The one who can stop Ignis."

"She is not that child," Frank said flatly.

I blinked. "How do you know?"

"Ages ago, when the Fae moved the stone into another realm to hide it, a chip broke off. A raven plucked it up then dropped it into the ocean. That chip, that piece of the Stone of Destiny, would choose the human child to help defeat the darkness, according to the prophecy."

Frank paused, leaning forward until his face was inches from mine.

I fought the urge to back away.

"And I believe that very stone is on a cord around your neck."

Behind me, Sean let out a cry of surprise, and Connor said something, too. But a dull rushing noise filled my ears as I groped for the fairy stone. No. This couldn't be right.

"It was my dad's," I found myself saying. "It's not really mine. It chose him, but he lost it."

"If that was the case, it was lost for good reason," Frank replied, straightening up and snapping his fingers to get the bartender's attention. "Nothing is a mistake with the Fae, girl."

The bartender set another pint of foamy black Guinness in front of Frank. He raised his glass in a toast, giving me another smirk. "May the Fae be with thee."

With that, he turned around and went back to his drink.

Stunned, I followed Sean and Connor out of the pub. Once we were back in the car, Connor started saying something to Eoin about trick-or-treating with friends in some neighborhood on the outskirts of Skullageen, and soon we were puttering down the road.

I stared numbly out of the window. This had to be a mistake. I couldn't be the child in the prophecy. I struggled to save myself from darkness—how could I possibly save the entire world?

The unicorn sign flashed by, and I stiffened in my seat. Next came the sign for the Goat and Clover pub.

"We'll hop out here," Connor said suddenly.

"Here?" Eoin sounded doubtful, but he pulled over. "Weird spot to go trick-or-treating."

"There's a good house right over that way," Connor said, already opening his door. "Rumor is they've got the best candy."

"Snickers bars," Sean added hastily. "The king-sized ones. American candy, too! Peanut butter cups. Solid gold candy corn. Bye!"

Connor elbowed Sean as they joined me on the sidewalk. "Solid gold candy corn?"

"Hey, it'd be worth the drive, wouldn't it?" Sean said. "Hey, Cara, wait up!"

I was already walking down the quiet country lane. Connor and Sean jogged to catch up with me. We passed a house with a rusty old kid's playground set in the yard. I spotted a chewed-up old tennis ball on the grass. It almost seemed to glow, and without thinking about it, I jogged over and picked it up.

"Uh . . ." Sean said as I stuck the ball in my jacket pocket.

"Don't ask," I muttered. I didn't feel like explaining that intuition told me I might need it.

"So are we gonna talk about what Frank said, or . . ." Connor trailed off, eyeing me.

"He said Ignis is Dubhan Lalor, like we thought," I replied as we started walking again. "The door to the Otherworld is on the factory site. It's the only other place I can think of that Bri would be."

"But Bri isn't the child in the prophecy—" Sean began, and I rounded on him.

"Yes she is! I don't care what Frank said about the fairy stone. Bri's the one who went mute. Bri's the one who keeps drawing everything before it happens. Bri's the one who found the Bow's comb. Don't you get it? It's *her,* not me, and I have to save her before Ignis gets to her!"

My voice had risen to an almost hysterical pitch. Before Connor or Sean could respond, I began walking even faster toward the site. The streetlights ended, and soon the only light was from the moon hanging low and yellow overhead. Connor flipped on the flashlight on his phone, and I saw the entrance to the building site.

"Someone's there," I said, my pulse quickening as I broke into a jog. "Bri? Bri, is that you?"

There were two figures facing one another alongside the chain-link fence. One had cat ears poking up, and I felt a surge of hope.

"Rose!" I cried, flat-out running now. "Did you find her?"

"Did you find her?" came a cruel, mocking voice.

I slowed down as Rose turned, her face going white at the sight of me. She stepped aside, and now I could see who she was with. Not Bri.

Rob Lalor.

He was in a grim reaper costume, Beast at his side. The dog snarled at me but made no move to come closer. Then I realized what Rob was doing. He wasn't just standing at the entrance. He was *blocking* the entrance. Him and his monstrous pooka dog.

He must have known we were coming. And there was only one person who could've told him. Rose hadn't texted her mom as we walked back from the shore.

She'd texted Rob.

"How could you?" I whispered, staring at her.

Rose ducked her head, her eyes filling with tears.

Dark, angry thoughts clouded my head. *You betrayed me. You're a coward. How could you?*

But I didn't say any of those thoughts out loud. *Shine bright,* I told myself. Rose's dad was out of work and angry, and he took it out on her. If he got a job at this factory, her life would be infinitely better. I couldn't forgive Rose, not right now. But I could try to understand. I could try to find the light.

Calm settled over me, and I stepped closer to Rob.

"Let me pass."

Rob snorted. "I think not."

"It's not your property."

"It's my dad's," Rob sneered. "Same thing."

"No." I crossed my arms. "It belongs to the Fae."

Rob let out a howl of laughter. "The Fae! You and your gran and your dumb, hippie rubbish—you're all useless. My dad's actually trying to *help* this community."

"Help?" Sean sputtered, and I realized he was right next to me. Connor stood on my other side, glaring at Rob. "Big help, building a plastics factory that'll destroy our ecosystem."

"Don't be such a nerd," Rob scoffed. "People need jobs. That's what matters. And—hey!"

I moved forward, but Rob quickly sidestepped, blocking my way onto site. He laughed, and slowly, I reached my hand into my jacket pocket and squeezed the ratty old tennis ball. I could feel Beast watching me intently. A low growl rumbled deep in his chest, but I kept my eyes on Rob. Behind him, the site was pitch-black, a field of muddy grass swallowed up in darkness.

"I'll ask you one more time," I said calmly. "Let me pass."

Rob smirked. "I'll tell you one more time . . . no."

"Have it your way."

I pulled the tennis ball from my pocket and hurled it at his face.

"Ah!" Rob stumbled back into the fence as the ball bounced off his forehead. Beast let out a bark and leaped for the ball—and I lunged for the entrance.

"Cara!" I heard Connor shouting in alarm. Sean was calling me, too, and Rob was cursing loudly over the sound of Beast's barks. I ran as fast as I could, my sneakers sticking in the mud. The sounds of their voices faded, but the barking was getting louder.

Beast was coming after me.

- SEVENTEEN -

The Portal

THE FIELD WAS BUMPY and rough. I slipped in a patch of mud and just barely managed not to fall. Beast abruptly stopped barking, but I didn't allow myself to slow down or look behind me. I raced across the muddy grass with only the moonlight to guide me.

Murky mist rolled in from all directions, forcing me to slow down. Then, not far behind me, I heard a deep, menacing growl that sounded as if it were coming from a creature much, much larger than Beast.

The Pooka, a shape shifting goblin . . . most often takes the form of a huge dog to accompany the Formor army, but it can change into anything a person fears.

The mist swirled around me, closing in on me, and I stopped running. A whimper escaped my throat as the darkness began to close in around my vision. Twisted faces with gaping mouths and long, wispy hands formed in the mist, silently screaming as they reached for me.

Keep moving, I told myself, and I took one step and then another. The growling stopped, but I knew the Pooka was still there. *Don't think about it. Just keep going.*

But even as I walked, I could tell I was going nowhere. Every few seconds, I could make out the outline of trees through the mist, but no matter which direction I walked, they never grew closer. I was trapped here.

"The stray!" I said suddenly. That's what Jimmy Jo had called it. A tricky Fae had put a stray on him so that he didn't know where he was, but he'd gotten home by . . . by what?

After a moment, I remembered. "My jacket!" I pulled it off and quickly turned it inside out, then slipped it back on. Then I started walking again, my heart hammering in my ears. After a few seconds, I spotted a stone wall with briars, and I sprinted for it.

Behind me came the *thump-thump-thump-thump* sound of an enormous animal running at full speed. Too terrified to scream, I reached the wall and tried to climb through the briars, thorns scratching my legs and arms. Then a deep, rattling growl caused me to freeze. I could feel the creature's hot breath as I slowly turned to face it.

A great, hulking shadow loomed before me, obscured by the mist. I gripped the fairy stone and lifted it to my eye—and felt my blood run cold.

The Pooka was easily the size of a lion, impossibly muscular and with eyes that glowed red like burning fire pits. It bared razor-sharp teeth as it took a slow, almost lazy step closer, and I dropped the stone back onto my chest.

I was paralyzed. *No escape. No hope.*

"No," I whispered, numb from head to toe. "I am a warrior of light."

Closing my eyes, I imagined myself glowing, a bright light illuminating the darkness around me. *Breathe in peace and calm, one, two, three, four . . . breathe out worry and fear, one, two, three, four, five, six . . .*

"You only have power if I give you power," I said, slightly louder. Then I opened my eyes and stared at the shadow beast. "You don't exist!"

An icy wind blew in, carrying a familiar wail. It grew louder and louder, and the Pooka's growls intensified. I stared, heart in my throat, as the Pooka stepped out of the mist—and then another creature bounded through the mist and shielded me.

I gaped at the enormous ashen Irish wolfhound.

The Bow sat atop the great dog, small and thin, her withered bluish skin exposed under the dark hooded cloak. She gripped a white wooden staff engraved with a serpent, raising it like the mightiest of warriors.

The Pooka snarled at the Bow. In response, she lifted her head and straightened her back. Then she thumped the staff hard into the earth.

The ground trembled, and the serpent engraving was infused with white light that unfurled and writhed up and down the staff. The Pooka snapped angrily, and the serpent suddenly hissed and lunged off the staff, clamping its jaws on the beast's leg.

The Pooka let out an otherworldly shriek, staggering back into the mist. Before I could react, the Bow grabbed the back of my shirt and pulled me up onto the wolfhound with astonishing strength.

The wolfhound took off, and I gripped the coarse fur at the nape of its neck tightly as we leaped over the scrub and across the field at lightning speed. I could hear the Bow's raspy breaths behind me, but I was no longer afraid of her. She helped me, just as she promised.

I let out a shriek as the wolfhound leaped over the stone wall, the ground falling away dizzyingly below us. We landed hard, and the wolfhound slowed to a halt.

I slid off, my limbs quaking uncontrollably, and looked up.

"Thank you," I whispered.

The Bow pushed back her hood. Her shining saucer eyes gleamed as she nodded. Then she tapped the wolfhound gently on the side with her staff, and they were off, disappearing into the darkness.

I stood there, still shivering, and tried to get my bearings. I appeared to be standing in a large rath, with a twisted hawthorn tree not far from me, a large boulder at its base. Other stones of various sizes were arranged around it in a circle.

Slowly, I walked over to the boulder. It came up to my waist, and I was shocked to realize there was a perfectly round hole right in the middle—like a giant fairy stone.

Disbelief and hope spread through me in equal measure. The Bow must have brought me here for a reason.

This was the door to the Otherworld!

Breathlessly, I dropped to my knees in the long grass and looked through the hole. For a moment, all I saw was the same grassy field. But then I noticed the faintest shimmer of light around the hole, as if the boulder itself was glowing.

There was only one way to find out whether this was the door. Taking a deep breath, I crawled through the hole.

Instantly, a warm breeze caressed my face. I got to my feet, feeling somehow lighter and smaller. The dark field was gone. Now, I stood in a woodland forest the likes of which I'd seen only in fantasy movies. The colors of the trees and grass and flowers were so vibrant, they seem to glow. In fact, even *I* glowed here! I gazed down at my arms in amazement, entranced by the golden sheen emanating from my skin.

Warmth and peace filled me for the first time since Dad disappeared. Utterly relaxed, I turned in a slow circle and spotted a stony path that led through the trees.

I strolled down the path, admiring the brilliant green vines wrapped around the tree trunks, and enormous white and yellow flowers with petals that felt like velvet. At last, the path ended at the base of the most extraordinary tree I had ever laid eyes on. It radiated every color of the rainbow, the bark pulsating and the colors flickering and changing before my eyes.

Everything here is made of light! I thought to myself, suddenly giddy with happiness. Then a faint but joyful voice reached my ears. Someone was singing.

"Oh, time to dance and let go of fear,
The season change is drawing near,
Time to rest beneath the earth,
Sit tight and wait for a brighter birth!"

I knew that voice! Peering around the tree, I spotted a spark of white light among a pile of shimmering golden leaves. I moved closer, watching as the spark gradually formed the shape of a golden leaf, dancing and twirling in the air.

As I knelt down, the leaf settled onto the forest floor and transformed into a tiny green acorn. It instantly sprouted little arms and legs and a face so delightful, I couldn't help but giggle. The acorn wore a tiny skull cap with a branch stork. Even though I had never laid eyes on it in this form, I knew where I'd heard that voice before.

"You were a robin," I said softly, leaning closer. "You spoke to me from the fairy tree in front of Granny's house. Y-you're a Fae."

The acorn tilted its face up at me. "I am an elemental, yes. My name is Jack."

"Jack, I'm Cara. I've come here to find my dad—Michael O'Reilly. He came to the Otherworld looking for the Stone of Destiny."

Jack's expression turned sad. "I'm afraid the one you seek is not here."

I swallowed hard. "What about my sister, Bri? She's eight years old—she has a raven familiar!"

Jack shook his tiny head, and I sighed, deflated. "Do you know where I can find the Stone of Destiny?"

"I must lay seeds for tomorrow." Jack suddenly busied himself scuttling around among the earth and leaves. He shimmered copper, yellow, and green, and I watched him for nearly a minute as if hypnotized. Then I snapped back to attention.

"Please, this is important! I need to find my dad and sister, and Ignis is trying to stop me. He's cursed my family!"

Jack gaped up at me. "Ignis, you say? A curse? Oh, there is not much time . . . I must find somewhere to bury myself so I may grow."

With that, he scurried away.

I hurried after him, feeling more desperate by the second. "Bury yourself? That won't do any good. Please, help me fight Ignis. Help me find the Stone of Destiny!"

"Finding the stone may be your duty, but alas, it is not mine!" he called. "We all have a part to play."

He came to a halt on a soft patch of warm brown earth and began to dig. I stared at him, my hand reaching into my rucksack and feeling beneath my tennis racket until I found the jam jar. My stomach churned with guilt, but I had no other choice.

Jack began to sing again as he burrowed into the dirt. "Jack rests beneath the earth, waiting for a brighter bir—hey!"

He looked up a split second before I lowered the jam jar down, trapping him inside.

EIGHTEEN

The Four
Treasures

Jack glared up at me, his tiny face screwed up in an indignant expression that would have been funny if I hadn't felt so terrible.

"Why do humans allow their sparkle to be clouded by fear?" he cried, throwing his arms up in exasperation. "Let life be!"

"I'm so sorry, Jack," I said desperately. "I hate doing this, but I can't just let things *be*. I have to take action, or Ignis will win."

With a heavy sigh, Jack sat down and folded his arms. "You are not here to help the Fae. You are no friend."

"I am, too!" I was starting to get frustrated. "I want to bring more sparkle into the world, just like you do. But I can't do it without the Stone of Destiny!"

"Be careful what you wish for," Jack muttered.

Keeping my hand on the top of the jam jar, I looked around for a path. "Which way do we go from here?"

Jack rolled his eyes. "A true warrior would know."

I opened my mouth to argue then remembered the fairy stone. Fumbling to pull the cord out from under my shirt, I dangled the stone in front of me.

A rainbow prism of light surrounded it, and a beam of light guided me onward, shimmering and wondrous. After scanning the area, I spotted a small sparkling door among the thick tangled roots of a towering oak. When I lowered the stone, I couldn't see it anymore. I placed the stone to my eye and peered through it, gazing at the door. It pulsated with a blue luminescent light.

Exhaling softly, I let the stone dangle once again in front of me as I turned my attention to another beam of light directed at a mossy bank beside a stream. Another door—only this one was a faded gray with white glimmers.

"I see two doors," I whispered, looking back and forth between them.

"There are many doors," Jack said, drumming his tiny fingers on the glass. "Each leading to a realm with varying degrees of light. Just like your world, shadow dwells. You must take the path that calls you. Use your insight but remember—looks can be deceptive."

"Well, that's easy enough," I said, scooping up the jar with Jack inside. "The blue door is much brighter."

I walked over to the oak tree then peered through the stone until I spotted the knob. I turned it slowly, and the door groaned open, revealing a narrow tunnel that led deep into the earth.

Lowering the stone, I picked up the jar. Jack covered his eyes as I tucked it safely into the side pocket of my rucksack. Then, steeling myself, I crawled inside.

The earth was moist and mossy, and after only a few seconds of wriggling on my belly, my shirt felt damp and cold. I crawled in silence for a full minute, then an odd scuffling sound caused me to freeze. A stench reached my nose, and I recoiled. It smelled sickly sweet, like rotting fruit.

Something else was in the tunnel with me.

I pulled my rucksack closer. "What is it?" I whispered to Jack.

"A Joint Eater," he replied matter-of-factly. "A creature that eats you from the inside."

I clamped a hand to my mouth, afraid I might retch. Then I tried to back up in the tunnel . . . only it was somehow even narrower now, and my shoulders stuck. I struggled for only a few seconds before falling still again. There was no going back.

The temperature dropped, and my body shivered violently.

Then a voice drifted down the tunnel, a screechy sound like nails on a chalkboard. "I can smell your fear. It's delicious."

Panic set in, and I squirmed backward, but that only wedged my shoulders tighter. "Jack, help me!" I cried, hoarse with fear.

But he didn't respond. Instead, the Joint Eater let out a cackle like shattering glass.

"There's no escape—you chose this path. Don't worry, it will all be over soon . . . once I suck that sparkle from your insides."

Bile burned in the back of my throat. I stopped struggling and tried to clear my thoughts of darkness. Squeezing the fairy stone, I held it out straight in front of me. *Breathe in calm . . . breathe out fear . . .*

The stone began to glow, faintly at first, then brighter. My breath caught in my throat as it illuminated the creature in the tunnel in front of me. It was eyeless, gray and slimy-skinned, with a wide mouth filled with razor teeth. As it inched closer, a cold horror unlike anything I'd ever felt before flooded through me.

"I can't," I gasped, and the light went out. Darkness surrounded me. "Jack, I can't . . . please . . ."

For a moment, he said nothing.

Of course he won't help me. I tricked him. I am darkness.

I closed my eyes and waited for the creature to take me.

Then, "Shadow creature, be *gone!*" Jack's voice rang out, strong and surprisingly commanding.

A flash of light blinded me, and I squeezed my eyes closed. When I opened them, the Joint Eater had vanished.

"Thank you," I said, shaking uncontrollably. "Thank you, Jack."

I crawled forward, desperate to get out of this tunnel, tiny bursts of light still twinkling around me. At last, I emerged into a clearing.

I collapsed onto the ground and lay there, still shaken by the encounter. A beautiful clearing surrounded me: emerald moss covered a forest floor scattered with glittering rocks and tiny, delicate flowers. Twisting tree branches covered with ivy formed a thick canopy overhead.

Setting my rucksack down, I took the jam jar out of the pocket.

Jack chuckled. "I think you need to work on your inner sight! That said, sometimes the hardest path brings the greatest light."

I stared down at the jam jar. I knew it was wrong to trap Jack, but I'd been desperate. I had tried to force him to help me. To control him. And that could only lead to darkness.

Reaching down, I unscrewed the jar lid.

"Thank you so much for helping me, Jack," I said softly. "I was wrong to capture you. Please, be free."

Gently, I lay the jar on its side. Jack walked out, gazing up at me with a peculiar expression. "We all have our duty, which must be carried out with kindness and humility. You have shown both of these qualities."

He walked toward a pile of leaves nearby. I watched as he climbed onto the pile and began burying himself in the earth. As he dug, white sparks sprayed from the ground. To my astonishment, Jack began to grow bigger . . . and bigger . . . and bigger.

Tree trunk legs and arms sprouted from his body, with branches for fingers and little roots for toes. A bushy ivy beard bloomed on his chin. Twigs burst from his forehead like antlers, and soft, springy moss covered his body like a green suit. When the transformation was complete, I leaned back in amazement, taking in this brilliant, enormous green creature of the forest.

Jack smiled down at me. "I have been waiting for you to prove yourself."

"You . . ." I paused, my mouth suddenly dry. "You were testing me?"

"Everything in life is a test. There are no mistakes. You see, while us Fae can see your sparkle, we can't easily see how much is obscured by darkness. You humans have willpower, so darkness can diminish . . . or grow. As a guardian of the forest realm, I had to be sure of your intentions."

I gaped at him. "Oh."

Around me, the ground began to sparkle. Except it wasn't ground, I realized with a start. I was kneeling on a large stone slab embedded in the forest floor. Wiping away a few leaves and vines, I saw markings etched into the stone, huge decorative swirls and embellishments. And not far from where I knelt, just at the edge of the stone, was a chip.

My heart fluttered in my chest, and my hand went instinctively to the fairy stone around my neck. I knew, without a doubt, that if I placed my stone into that chip, it would be the perfect fit. Which meant—

"This is the Stone of Destiny," I whispered.

As if in response, the stone trembled.

I scrambled to my feet as the entire forest seemed to rumble.

"It's woken up," Jack announced. "Your pure intentions have revealed what you desire . . . it lies beneath your feet."

The rumbling and trembling ceased, and I stared down at the stone, trying to catch my breath.

"The Stone of Destiny is one of the four treasures of our people," Jack went on. "Each treasure holds the power of pure light, which helps dispel darkness. Each was hidden to protect that power. Those markings you see are an ancient language . . . the etching here means *one*. Those who stand upon the stone find unity, not separation."

Warmth radiated from the stone, spreading up my legs and into my chest and head. I suddenly felt as though I might float away.

Jack smiled. "The stone will allow you to ask me one question, and it will grant you one wish."

One question. The words flew from my mouth before I could second-guess it. Because what other question could I ask, other than the one that had dominated my thoughts for a week?

"Where is my dad?"

Jack's face softened. "I'm afraid your father is no longer a part of your world. He has begun his journey into the world of pure light."

The words took a few seconds to sink in. I shook my head violently. "No. He's not . . . do you mean he's—is he *dead*?"

Jack bowed his head. "Yes."

Grief ripped through me, more agonizing than anything I had ever felt. I fell to my knees on the stone and wept bitterly. All this time, Connor was right. The Fae were real after all, but I had been clinging to the stories to avoid facing the truth: Dad couldn't have survived on that trail during such a terrible storm. I had been deluding myself, thinking I felt a connection with him in Granny's study, even at Coffin Rock.

This is why Bri can't talk, I thought, lost in despair. *She's known all along that Dad didn't make it. She couldn't find the words to tell us.*

"I thought I could find him," I said through hiccups and sobs. "I should have known I couldn't . . . that it was all my fault . . . that he's dead b-because of me—"

"What makes you believe such a thing?" Jack asked softly.

"I was angry with him the day he left to climb the mountain. I blamed him for working so much. I was mad that he missed my tennis tournament . . . I was so angry that I wished him *gone*." I wiped my cheeks, hot with shame and regret. "Dad always warned me that my thoughts had power. He was right. I made this happen."

"Cara, thoughts only hold power for the person thinking them," Jack said. "It was your father's time to go. Death is one of the great mysteries. You can't change another person's destiny."

I blinked away more tears. "Did Ignis kill him?"

Jack gave me an apologetic look. "I can only answer one question, Cara."

One question . . . and one wish.

I sucked in a sharp breath, struggling to get to my feet. I stared down at the stone, squeezed my hands into fists, and said, "I wish the day my dad died never happened! I wish he'd never gone off to climb that stupid mountain!"

Nothing happened.

Jack sighed. "Wishes, much like earthly happenings, cannot go backward. Only forward."

I stamped my foot angrily. "But I want him back! I want everything back the way it was!"

"Just as the river flows toward the sea, life can only go onward." Jack took a step closer. "Yet it is also true that how you look at the world shapes it. Your father lives on in your heart . . . who he truly is can never die. Your quest, just like his, holds great possibility. Be compassionate with yourself, Cara. Do that, and all will be well."

But I didn't feel compassion toward myself. I blamed myself. I *should* blame myself. Nothing would ever be well again. Not without Dad.

The glittering light of the clearing began to fade. Darkness rolled in like a fog, blackening the trees, their branches curling and twisting and reaching for me like claws. Only now, I didn't feel fear. I was too lost in grief.

"Ignis is here," Jack warned. "Cara, you must let your sparkle shine!"

Black ivy and thorny brambles wrapped around my ankles and pulled tight. I fell forward, landing hard on the stone. I could feel Jack doing his best to free me from their grip, but it was no use . . .

Blindly, I reached for the fairy stone. *Breathe in calm. Breathe out fear.*

I thought of Dad. His smile, his twinkling eyes, the way he laughed. And once again, I felt that connection with him, with his love—because death couldn't destroy that connection. Nothing could. Wherever my father was now, he was still in my heart and always would be.

You are light, Cara, he whispered in my head.

"I am light," I whispered out loud.

And just like that, I knew my wish.

- NINETEEN -

Hag's Rock

I WISH TO BRING *more sparkle into the world!*" The moment the words left my lips, I felt the ivy and brambles release their grip on me. Warmth flooded through me as I got to my feet. A shimmering glow enveloped me, and I closed my eyes briefly and smiled as I heard Dad's voice one last time.

You are a warrior of light, Cara. Go forth with this power and fight the darkness.

When I opened my eyes, Jack was watching me with a pleased expression.

"Well done," he said. "Now, we have to be quick—Ignis will try to stop you leaving with the fairy stone. This way."

I followed Jack to an enormous tree leaning so far over to the side, its topmost branches grazed the forest floor. Jack pushed aside a loose root, revealing a hole in the ground. I thought of the Joint Eater then pushed that thought away firmly. In a flash, Jack transformed into a robin and flew into the hole. I followed without hesitation.

Spiderwebs brushed my face, and once or twice I felt a tiny bug scuttle across my hand. Gritting my teeth, I kept going.

When we emerged on the other side, a gust of wind nearly knocked me off my feet. Jack perched on my arm, and we stared at the breathtaking sight in front of us.

We stood at the edge of a cliff. Far below, the ocean was a frantic swirl of crashing, foaming waves. The drop was so dizzying, I had to turn away.

I found myself facing a huge, ragged rock shaped almost like a hunched old woman. Thunder boomed in the distance, and the sky was quickly darkening. I reached for Jack as the ragged rock began to vibrate then shake violently. There was a *snap,* and a crack appeared down the center . . . and then another and another. To my astonishment, the rock cracked like an egg in front of my eyes, stone crumbling to the ground.

And there, in the center of the rubble, was a tiny, fragile figure. I knew instantly what it was, but I could hardly believe what I was seeing.

"Is that . . . a baby?" I managed to say.

Jack patted my hand with his claw. "Yes and no. That is no ordinary baby, Cara. She is the Fae queen Brigid."

My mouth fell open. The baby looked like a newborn—as tiny as my little brother had seemed when I'd first seen him in my mother's arms.

"It's Hag's Rock," I said softly, remembering Dad's story. *The Formors imprisoned her sparkle in Hag's Rock. When Brigid is born on Halloween, her sparkle is released from the rock, and she grows older and stronger through spring and summer just like everything in the seasons, working hard to help the earthly realm before her strength fades again.*

A bolt of lightning flashed across the sky. Heavy droplets of rain began to fall, quickly picking up speed. In seconds, I was drenched and freezing.

"Ignis and his shadow army grow closer!" Jack cried. "He's coming. Get Brigid!"

I was already running toward the infant. Another bolt of lightning sliced through the air, hitting the ground so close to me that I let out a scream and stopped dead, staring at the black, scorched grass. The baby began to wail.

I can't do this. I don't want this responsibility. It's too hard. It's too dangerous.

I took a step back, shivering and ready to flee. Then I caught myself.

"Ignis, I know you're messing with my thoughts," I said out loud. "But you won't stop me!"

Hurrying forward, I pulled off my inside-out jacket and scooped the infant up gently, wrapping her up as best I could.

Her small, beautiful face was streaked with rain and tears, but she smiled up at me and cooed.

I touched her nose and smiled. "Don't worry, little one. I'll keep you safe."

"Cara!"

I turned around and spotted Jack perched on a small rock, looking at me impatiently.

"This way, through the gate!"

He took off, soaring to a small red metal gate in the distance. I ran after him as fast as I could, clutching the baby to my chest. The wind picked up, and the raindrops turned to hail, pelting my face and arms and leaving tiny, stinging red welts. I shielded the baby's face with my arm . . . and suddenly, I remembered Bri's drawing.

The girl holding the baby. I had thought the girl in that drawing was Bri herself—the human child from the prophecy. But now I knew the truth.

Bri had drawn *me*. All this time, she knew I was the child destined to save the world from Ignis. She had seen me holding the newborn Brigid.

I really and truly was the child in the prophecy!

Fresh adrenaline coursed through my veins, my purpose driving me forward. I reached the gate and lifted the latch, keeping a tight grip on the baby with my other arm. Another bolt of lightning hit, this one so close it singed my hair. I yanked the gate open and sprinted down a narrow path in the dark. More lightning lit up the sky, and I could just make out the neat rows of rocks in the grass on either side of me.

Not rocks. Tombstones.

I was running straight through a cemetery.

As the tombstones started to tremble, I came to a halt. Bri's picture . . . blood rushed in my ears as I remembered the giant, macabre creature made of skulls.

I swiveled around, intending to run back through the gate, as far away from these buried bones as I could. But the gate was gone. I was surrounded by graves, and the earth shook hard beneath my feet. There was nowhere to run now.

Ignis was here.

- TWENTY -

The Bone Man

J ACK FLITTED PAST my ear, causing me to shriek. I heard his shout faintly beneath the storm.

"Take cover in Kilcatherine's church!"

Dread mounted inside me as I spun around and spotted the ruined church on top of the hill. Thunder cracked, and seconds later, a spiderweb of lightning lit up the sky, offering me a terrifying view of hundreds of tombstones rattling in the earth like loose teeth. I slipped and slid in the mud, fighting to make my way up the hill. The baby squirmed in my arms, and though it was impossible, I couldn't help thinking she was getting heavier and larger by the second.

Jack flew ahead.

"Where now?" I shouted at Jack over the howl of the wind.

"You must find Brigid's door!"

Frustration bubbled up inside of me. "Another test, really? Just tell me, please!"

But Jack had already flown off, leaving me alone with Brigid.

My arms ached, and I knelt down and laid her on the grass. When I unwrapped the jacket, I reeled back in shock.

It hadn't been my imagination—the infant had grown into a toddler! She sat up and beamed at me, the rain plastering her long dark hair to her forehead. As I watched in disbelief, Brigid pulled herself to her feet and took one tottery step, then another.

I stood, too, grabbing my jacket and putting it back on. I followed Brigid as she toddled through the graveyard, increasingly sure-footed with every step—until suddenly, she plopped down in the mud and began to wail.

"Brigid!" I cried, rushing forward and scooping her up—and then I froze.

Something was emerging from the ground in front of us. Something ivory white and spider-like.

A skeleton hand.

"No, no, no," I moaned, stepping backward—*crunch!*

Shrieking, I leaped away in horror. I had stepped on another hand, snapping it in two. But the pieces rejoined, and the bony hand began scuttling toward my feet.

I jumped out of its way, but then I saw more skeleton hands emerging from their graves, followed by arms, torsos, legs, feet . . .

skulls. The parts were all separated, and they moved like creatures from a nightmare, wriggling, clawing, squirming through the mud.

They all moved toward an ancient tomb, drawn as if by a magnet. And as they reached the tomb, the bony parts began to join to one another: hand to foot, knee to rib, spine to skull, a skeleton mishmash that grew and grew and *grew.*

As Brigid's wails grew louder, Jack landed on my shoulder. "Ignis is shape-shifting," he said softly.

I was too horrified to answer, entranced by the expanding monstrous mass of bones. As I watched, that mass formed a torso, two thick limbs extending as legs, then two more as arms. Finally, dozens of skulls rolled up to the very top and banded together to form a head with a single empty black eye socket and a gaping void of a mouth.

A thick, gray fog rolled in. I couldn't take my eyes off the ever-growing bone man—but then shadows in the mist finally got me to tear my gaze away.

More creatures were emerging, gorilla-like and menacing, twisted goat horns atop their heads. Some swung wooden clubs or swords; others gripped chain leashes attached to snarling Pookas. The graveyard was suddenly filled with awful, animalistic grunts, punctuated with the occasional roar.

I didn't need Jack to explain what I was seeing. The Formor army had arrived.

The bone man's mouth opened wider. When it spoke, its voice—Ignis's voice—was like a cacophony of screams and shouts that ranged from ear-splittingly high-pitched to a low drone that rumbled deep in my gut.

"I feed on your fear. Even now, see how I grow?"

This was followed by a laugh so awful I ducked my head and fell to my knees. Brigid's scream was lost to the sound of the wind and the Formor army's howls and roars.

Spots danced in front of my eyes. I couldn't defeat such evil. It was impossible. I was just one girl up against a shadow army.

Shadow army.

I fought off the darkness threatening to consume me and tried to think. Shadows were just an illusion. Ignis was a trick-ster, feeding off my fear to grow stronger—so I couldn't let him have my fear. I had to be the light.

Boom.

My head jerked up. Ignis had begun to move, one earth-shaking step after another. In his right hand, he gripped a massive club made entirely out of femurs. He swung it back and forth, and I ducked as giant chunks of tombstones went flying.

"Your father couldn't stop me, and neither will you!"

He began making his way toward me, that empty eye socket fixing on my face.

Balor of the evil eye.

The story Granny had told Bri and me—my father's favorite story—rushed back into my mind. And suddenly, I knew exactly what I had to do.

"It's hopeless, little girl. Darkness is upon your realm."

I ignored him, carefully setting Brigid on the ground before unzipping my rucksack and pulling out my tennis racket. Then I yanked the cord from my neck and gripped the fairy stone. "You and your shadows have no power if I don't give you power."

Ignis came to a halt, glowering down at me.

I lifted my chin and looked directly into his dark, evil eye. *Breathe in calm. Breathe out fear.*

"Balor was defeated," I said, loudly and clearly. "And so, too, are you!"

I tossed the fairy stone up then swung the racket as hard as I could. *Thwack!*

The stone arced high into the air, a perfect serve. I held my breath as it soared toward that hideous bone face . . . and vanished into that cavernous black eye.

The scream of fury Ignis let out shook the earth, causing the Formor army to retreat back into the mist. I staggered backward as the bone man began to tremble, a few skulls clattering down its body—and then it collapsed into a heap of bones with a deafening crash.

The rain slowed, and the clouds began to part, revealing a deep blue sky. As the mist receded into the trees, I heard the last few, faint roars of the Formor army as they vanished.

I stood there in disbelief. Had I really defeated Ignis? Was it all finally over?

Brigid leaped to her feet and sprinted toward the stone archway of the ruined church with a swiftness no toddler possessed.

My gaze moved from her to the archway, and I spotted a stone carving of a woman's face. "Brigid's door," I whispered, and I took off after her.

- TWENTY-ONE -

Brigid

A SERENE SILENCE HUNG in the church. I slowed to a halt, taking in the dark wooden pews, the stone altar and mahogany pulpit, the way early morning light streamed in through the stained glass windows, creating a dazzling kaleidoscope effect that took my breath away.

I began to move slowly down the aisle. "Brigid?" I called softly. "Where are you?"

"Here."

A young girl stepped out from behind the pulpit, smiling almost shyly at me. Dark curls framed her round face, and her eyes sparkled with something close to mischief.

I stared at her, stunned. She looked so much like Bri that for a moment, I thought my little sister had somehow found her way into the church while I battled Ignis.

"Uh, hi," I said finally, and immediately felt foolish.

Brigid's smile widened. "I want to thank you for your bravery, Cara. You fulfilled the prophecy, and I know it was no easy task."

I pushed my wet hair out of my eyes. "I can't believe it's over," I said. "Ignis is really gone."

"Ah." A cloud passed over Brigid's face. "He is gone . . . for now. His defeat is only temporary."

I shivered. "But he lost the Stone of Destiny. I found it. I released its sparkle."

Brigid stepped closer, clasping her hands together as if in prayer. She was still growing, still aging, transforming from a girl to a young woman in front of my eyes.

"You did," Brigid said. "But remember, the Stone of Destiny is just one of the four Fae treasures. Ignis will no doubt go after the others next." She caught the look on my face and smiled encouragingly. "But I have faith you will protect those, too, Cara."

Behind her, sunlight suddenly streamed through the stained glass windows at the front of the church. I threw my hand up, shielding my eyes from the blinding array of colors.

"What are the other three treasures?" I asked desperately. "Where are they? How do I protect them?"

I could barely make out Brigid's silhouette now, surrounded by a rainbow of light.

"You will know when the time comes," she said, her voice fading. She reached out her hand and placed the fairy stone in mine. "You are a warrior of light, Cara."

I squeezed my eyes shut as the light flashed bright white—then it was gone.

Neon spots danced in my vision as I blinked rapidly, staring around for Brigid. But the church was empty now, the rainbow lights gone. After a long moment, I turned and walked out of the church.

Ignis was still out there, planning his next move. But I had won the first battle. I found the Stone of Destiny and saved the world from the Formor army and eternal darkness—at least, temporarily.

And if I could do it once, I could do it again.

I trudged across the muddy field toward the chain-link fence, lost in thought. Distantly, I heard someone shouting my name. I looked up, and my heart skipped a beat.

There were Connor and Sean, waving their arms to get my attention. Behind them, I saw a familiar car parked along the curb. The doors flew open, and out spilled Aunt Jackie, Uncle Pat . . . and Bri.

My hand flew to my mouth as our eyes locked. Then Bri broke into a run, and so did I.

I let out a sob of relief as Bri threw her arms around me, nearly knocking me over. She wept into my shoulder, and I squeezed her as tight as I could.

"It's okay," I whispered. "Everything's going to be okay." And for the first time since Dad had disappeared, I believed it.

- TWENTY-TWO -

The Wish

MORNING SUNLIGHT WARMED my face. I kept my eyes closed, still half asleep and cocooned in soft blankets, wondering what time it was.

Gradually, I became aware of a light clicking sound. Yawning deeply, I rubbed my eyes and squinted as the room came into focus. Then I sat up straight. "Granny!"

Granny looked up from her knitting and beamed at me, her needles pausing over a half-finished blue scarf. "Cara, sweetheart! Sleep well?"

I nodded. "You look so much better!" I couldn't believe the difference. The color had returned to Granny's cheeks, and her eyes were sharp and clear.

"I *feel* so much better." Granny set the needles down in her lap. "Thanks to you. Had quite an adventure last night, did you?"

My chest squeezed as everything came flooding back—the terrifying bone creature, the Formor army, Ignis's cruel voice, Brigid . . .

"Bri!" I looked over at her bed then relaxed when I saw she was curled up beneath her duvet. "I thought I'd lost her, Granny. She disappeared after I returned the comb to the Bow, and I thought she was the child in the prophecy, I was so worried . . ."

I trailed off, looking uncertainly at Granny. Was she about to accuse me of making up stories?

"You were worried about your sister, and your sister was worried about you." Granny smiled softly over at Bri. "She rode her bike all the way to Jimmy Jo's for help."

I blinked in surprise. "Jimmy Jo? Why him?"

"Well, I think it was because she thought he was the only adult who would believe her when she claimed her sister was about to fight Ignis and the Formor army."

Granny fell silent for a moment, gazing down at her hands.

I held my breath and waited for her to continue.

"My fault," she said softly. "I never should have pretended not to believe in the Fae, and I never should have convinced Jackie to do the same. We were just trying to protect you children. Instead, you felt you couldn't come to us for help when you needed it most."

I sat back against my pillows, suddenly feeling as if an enormous weight had been lifted off my shoulders. "It's okay, Granny," I told her. "Really. I understand."

Granny sighed. "It all worked out, thanks to you. And when Bri showed Jimmy Jo her drawings, he knew immediately what was happening. He contacted Jackie, and she headed straight out to get Bri and go find you." Her voice caught, and tears sparkled in her eyes. "But you had already faced Ignis . . . and won. I'm so very proud of you, Cara. And I know your father would be, too."

My eyes burned with tears, too. "Thank you," I whispered, throwing off the blankets and hurrying over to give her a hug. Granny held me for a long time, both of us crying quietly.

"Why the sob fest?"

The sound of a gruff voice down by my feet caused me to jump. I looked down to see Hugo the hedgehog glaring up at me.

"Watch your step there, missy!" he said, waving a tiny fist.

"Hey, now," Granny chided him. "I may have been ill, but don't think I didn't hear my granddaughter come ask you for help—and you turned her down! Too old for quests, are you?"

Hugo sniffed. "I am. Adventures are for the young."

"Well now, if that isn't the biggest load of nonsense I've ever heard . . ." Granny muttered. I stifled a giggle as Hugo crossed his little arms.

"I didn't see you leaping out of bed to help!"

"I was cursed!" Granny gave him a pointed look.

Hugo made a small huffing sound. "Excuses, excuses." And with that, he turned in a few circles, curled up, and went to sleep.

"Anyway." Granny turned her attention back to me. "I got some news this morning. First, about Brian Lalor's factory."

My head jerked up. "He's not still building it, is he?"

"I managed to get someone from town hall on the phone," Granny said. "I told them my granddaughter had discovered an ancient site on those grounds while trick-or-treating." She gave me a wink. "They promised to send someone from Irish heritage to assess it. It's highly unlikely the factory will go ahead when they do."

I breathed a sigh of relief. Then I thought of Rose, and a little knot tightened in my stomach. I wasn't sure if I could forgive her for betraying me last night, but she didn't deserve to live with an angry and abusive father.

"What about all the jobs?" I asked. "A lot of people were hoping to work at the factory."

"Oh, I think they'll be fine," Granny said with a smile. "After all, when the site is confirmed a historical landmark, it will attract more tourists to the area, and that always leads to more jobs in the community."

The knot loosened a tiny bit. I hoped Rose's father would be able to get one of those jobs.

"The church," I said suddenly, looking up at Granny. "Kilcatherine's church is in the background of that photo of you in the Ballymore Grove of the Druids! Did you know the factory site was where the door to the Otherworld was all along?"

"Goodness, no," Granny said, shaking her head. "I suspect there are many undiscovered sites and doors in this area, but I never dreamed we were so close to a door. Nor did Frank, I'm sure."

Many undiscovered sites. I couldn't help but think of the three remaining Fae treasures Brigid had mentioned.

"Now, the other news." Granny's smile faded. "I had a call from the rescue team this morning."

My throat tightened. I knew what she was going to say, and I didn't want her to have to say it. "They found him," I whispered.

Granny squeezed her eyes closed, her face a mask of grief. "They did."

We sat in silence for a long moment. Then Granny stood and came over to sit next to me. She wrapped her arm around me, and I leaned into her and allowed myself to weep.

The grief was like an iron weight on my heart. But there was also relief that the endless waiting was finally over. Now, my family could begin to heal.

Mom arrived that afternoon.

Bri and I flew outside the moment we heard the car rumbling up the driveway. When it rolled to a stop, the driver's door opened, and Mom stepped out. She fell to her knees and spread her arms out wide, and my sister and I ran straight into her embrace.

The next few days were spent planning Dad's wake and funeral. But there was light to balance the darkness. My mother was sad, but she was also herself again. Bri was still mute, but she smiled more frequently now.

And then there was my baby brother, who had my dad's eyes. I spent as much time holding him as I could, gazing down at his perfect little face.

"I haven't found the right name for him yet," Mom said. She was curled up in Granny's armchair, a mug of tea cradled in her hands.

After a big family dinner, we were all gathered in the living room together: Aunt Jackie and Uncle Pat on the couch, Granny in her rocking chair, and Bri, Connor, and me cross-legged on the rug in front of the fireplace. I held my brother in my lap, wrapped in a soft green blanket.

"I'm sure we'll come up with one soon," Granny said. "Something just right for a boy who will no doubt grow up to be a brave, strong warrior like his big sisters!"

I blushed, ducking my head.

Mom cleared her throat. "For the last few days, you all have been hinting about some grand adventure," she said wryly. "Would anyone like to fill me in?"

All eyes immediately fell on me, and I felt my face heat up even more.

"I'll tell you," I said finally. "But first, I should warn you . . . it's about the Fae."

Mom laughed. "Of course it is. Your father would be thrilled."

Her voice broke slightly, and I swallowed hard.

Then I told my family the whole story.

No one spoke the entire time I talked. By the time I finished, my throat felt raw and scratchy. For a moment, the only sound in the living room was the crackle of the fire.

Then Mom took a deep breath. "Michael would be so, so very proud of you, Cara. Both of you," she added to Bri.

I wiped my eyes hastily, glancing around. Everyone was crying—even Connor's eyes were suspiciously red.

"So does that mean you believe in fairies now?" I asked Mom teasingly, trying to lighten the mood.

She let out a little laugh. "Anything's possible."

My brother let out a little coo, and Mom looked at him. A smile tugged at the corner of her mouth.

"You know, Cara," she said softly. "I think he liked your story. And I think maybe we've found the right name."

"Really?" I asked. "What is it?"

"Jack."

Immediately, I pictured Jack—not the robin, not the giant man of the forest, but the way he'd looked when I'd first found him, a perfect little acorn with a cherub's face.

"Jack," I repeated, laughing when my brother took hold of my pinkie with his tiny fingers. "It's perfect."

At the wake the next day, we all shared stories about Dad. I talked about how much I loved it when he pretended to be a monster at bedtime. I would hide in my bedroom, waiting for him to find me. When he did, he would tickle me relentlessly as I squealed with delight.

When it was Bri's turn, she showed us a drawing of Dad up in the sky, radiating sun rays down on us.

Dozens of people showed up for the funeral. I sat in the front pew of the church next to Mom, hardly hearing a word of the sermon. I couldn't take my eyes off the coffin that held my father. Before the burial, we formed a single file line and walked past it to say our final goodbyes.

I put my hand on the coffin and closed my eyes tight.

I didn't mean the things I said to you the last time I saw you. I love you so much.

My fingers found the fairy stone around my neck, and I squeezed it hard. I could practically see Dad smiling at me, and though I couldn't hear his voice anymore, I knew what he would say.

It was never your fault, Cara. Forgive yourself.

I nodded, my throat tight with tears.

When I moved away to let Bri have her goodbye, Aunt Jackie pulled me into a hug.

"Life won't be the same without him," she whispered in my ear. "But we will find a way to live with this loss. Here."

Pulling away, she pressed a purple ribbon into my hand.

I wiped my eyes and looked up at her. "What's this for?"

"It's a wish," she said, squeezing my shoulder. "Tie it to the fairy tree and it's bound to come true."

After the burial, we returned to the farmhouse, and Granny pulled platters of mini-sandwiches and quiches and pies from the fridge. As the adults sipped coffee and chatted in the living room, I joined Connor and Sean out on the porch.

Sean smoothed his hair down when he saw me, his expression nervous. "I'm really sorry about your dad, Cara."

"Thanks." I smiled, sitting down on the stoop next to him. "It was nice of you to come today."

"I'm sorry, too," Connor said. "Not just about Uncle Michael, but . . . but for not believing you. I never should have doubted you, Cara."

I looked at him in surprise. "It's okay! I know how ridiculous it all must've sounded. I didn't believe it either until I saw the Bow."

The front door opened and closed, and the three of us turned to see Bri. She held a piece of paper out to me, and I took it and held it out so Connor and Sean could see, too.

It was a drawing of four warriors, arms raised in triumph.

"Whoa, is that us?" Sean cried. "We look like superheroes!"

"We are!" I said, grinning up at Bri. "We defeated Ignis together."

She beamed at me then turned and headed back inside the house.

He is gone . . . for now. His defeat is only temporary.

A shiver ran through me as Connor and Sean continued talking about the drawing. I couldn't forget what the Fae queen Brigid had said. There were still three Fae treasures out there, and Ignis would no doubt go after them. I had no idea where they were, or even *what* they were.

Suddenly, I got to my feet.

"Cara, where are you going?" Connor asked as I hurried down the porch steps.

"To make a wish!" I called back.

I pulled the purple ribbon Aunt Jackie had given me from my pocket and stopped in front of the fairy tree. Colorful ribbons and glittering trinkets swayed in the breeze. Carefully, I tied the ribbon around a branch and made my wish.

I wish to bring more sparkle into the world so it is free from darkness for good.

My purple ribbon fluttered when I let go. I took a deep breath, touching the fairy stone around my neck. *Breathe in love . . . breathe out sadness . . .*

Somewhere out there, Ignis was plotting his next move. But when he made it, I would be ready.

I would shine bright.

Made in United States
Troutdale, OR
10/09/2023

13535732R20141